THE COST
OF CLAIMING
HIS HEIR

THE COST
OF CLAIMING
HIS HEIR

MICHELLE SMART

MILLS & BOON

First published in Great Britain 2020
by Mills & Boon, an imprint of HarperCollins*Publishers*
1 London Bridge Street, London, SE1 9GF
www.harpercollins.co.uk

HarperCollins *Publishers*
1st Floor, Watermarque Building, Ringsend Road
Dublin 4, Ireland

Large Print edition 2021

© 2020 Michelle Smart

ISBN: 978-0-263-28847-6

MIX
Paper from
responsible sources
FSC™ C007454

Printed and bound in Great Britain
by CPI Group (UK) Ltd, Croydon, CR0 4YY

CHAPTER ONE

THE ROAR FROM the watching crowd was deafening. Becky Aldridge, wiping tables in a deserted hospitality marquee, guessed Emiliano Delgado, owner and player of the Delgado team, had scored. Whenever the Delgado team had played during the past three weeks of the cup competition the spectating crowd had tripled. Becky had started work there knowing nothing of the polo world. She still knew nothing of the game, but of its star player she'd learned a lot. Mostly that everyone fancied him.

Carrying the last of the dirty glasses to the bar, she realised she had company: two dogs happily scooping up chips and other goodies carelessly dropped on the grass.

'Jenna?' she called out, and was not in the least surprised to receive no reply. Jenna, who was supposed to be manning the bar with Becky, had done another disappearing act, no doubt to watch the ongoing semi-final. Jenna was a major Emiliano Delgado groupie and the font of all Becky's knowledge of the half-Spanish, half-Argentinian billionaire hunk.

After checking that none of the handful of people mooching about outside the marquee were the owners of the dogs, Becky approached the pair armed with tiny chunks of hotdog sausages to tempt them. It worked. The dogs acted as if they were old friends, tails wagging and happily eating off her hand. Supplying them with a bowl of water, she took a seat at one of the outside tables and dialled the number that was on both their collars. It went straight to a generic voicemail.

'Hi, my name's Becky, and you can stop panicking because I've got your dogs with me. I work in the hospitality marquee opposite the fairground. It's the marquee with the pink roof, so you should find me easily enough, but if you get lost just call me back. I'll look after them until you get here. Okay then, bye.'

Throughout her rambling message, the two dogs sat and watched her. They really were gorgeous things. The bigger one was a golden retriever with dopey eyes, the smaller one a beautiful mongrel.

'Don't worry,' she told them as she stroked their heads, 'I'm sure your mummy or daddy will be here for you soon.'

A thirsty passer-by entered the tent. Becky's worries about what to do with the dogs were quickly dispelled when they followed her to the bar. Indeed, so obedient were they that when she commanded them to stay in a hidden corner of the bar area they curled up together and kept a watchful eye on her.

Half an hour passed. Jenna returned mere seconds ahead of the next influx of customers. The match had finished, with the Delgado team winning the semi-final six-five, and the boisterous crowd was keen to celebrate. So busy did the hospitality tent get that Becky could only give the dogs the odd pat on the head here and there and sneak the odd bit of hotdog to them.

'What the hell are they doing here?'

In the midst of pouring five pints of lager for a rowdy group of young men and trying to tune out that they were all ogling her breasts, Becky hadn't noticed the manager's return. Mark was looking at the dogs as if they were the carriers of disease.

'They appeared during the last match,' she explained over the noise. 'I've left a message with their owner.'

'They can't stay here.'

'Why not? We don't prepare food in here.'

'This isn't ruddy doggy day-care. Get rid of them.'

Placing the third pint glass in front of the customer, she immediately started pouring another. 'They've lost their owner.'

'I don't care. Get rid of them.'

'Let me finish doing this round and then I'll take them outside and wait for the owner.'

'No, you'll get rid of the flea-ridden mutts and get back to work.'

'Have a heart,' she beseeched, knowing as she spoke that she was wasting breath. Mark had proved in her short time there that he didn't have a heart. 'I'm sure…'

He grabbed her arm tightly and snarled into her ear, '*I'm* sure that if you want to keep your job you'll do as you're…'

A low growl cut Mark off mid-flow. The smaller of the dogs had joined them and was sitting on its haunches beside Becky, staring at the manager with its teeth bared.

Whether he did it reflexively or deliberately Becky could never be certain, but Mark's reaction to the small dog growling at him was to kick it. The dog yelped. Becky's reaction to this cruelty was instinctive and immediate; she threw the full pint she'd just finished pouring straight into her boss's face.

The marquee fell into silence.

His face like an overripe beetroot, Mark wiped the lager off his face with his hands. '*Bitch.*'

Outraged at Mark's despicable actions, Becky scooped the whimpering hound into her arms. 'You kicked a defenceless dog, you monster.'

'You're fired.'

'I don't care. You're despicable and I'm going to report you.'

Through all the flurry of drama, Becky had failed to notice the reason for the crowd's fall into silence, and that was the tall, lean figure dressed in the Delgado team green and white striped polo shirt, streaked with mud, who'd made his way to the front of the bar and was staring at Mark with unmistakable loathing. 'You kicked my dog?'

Mark, recognising him, paled. 'It was more of a tap,' he mumbled.

Becky, too distressed and angry to care that the great Emiliano Delgado had appeared or that Jenna was having palpitations beside her, kept careful hold of the dog while she wiped a tear away. 'He *did*,' she said. 'He was shouting at me, and this gorgeous boy—' she kissed the top of the dog's head '—was trying to protect me, and Mark kicked him.'

There was a moment of stillness as Emiliano looked from Becky and the dog to the now cowering Mark. And then he pounced. With an agility that belied his size, Emiliano vaulted over the bar, grabbed Mark by the scruff of the neck and proceeded to drag him out of the marquee.

As the golden retriever decided to follow his master, Becky hurried after him with the mongrel still in her arms, and got the retriever to heel.

In the open air, Emiliano threw Mark to the ground. 'I should kick *you*,' he raged as he loomed over him, 'see how you like being kicked, but you're not worth it. Now I suggest you leave before I change my mind. You can consider yourself fired.'

'You can't...' But, with one look at Emiliano's face, Mark quickly stopped his protest to cover his own face.

Emiliano laughed menacingly. 'If I say you're fired, you're fired.' Then, turning to the breathless, heavily made-up woman in hot pants and a vest who'd just run up to join him, he said, 'And you're fired too. I pay you to look after Rufus and Barney for me. They escaped on your watch.'

The woman's face paled as quickly as Mark's had done. 'It was an accident,' she pleaded.

'An accident because you were too busy trying to get into Juan's jodhpurs to pay attention to them. Anything could have happened. Get out of my sight.'

And then he turned to Becky, who'd watched the exchange with fascination.

The retriever nuzzled against her leg. The mongrel licked her face. She wondered if they were sympathising for the tongue-lashing she was about to receive for not taking better care of them—after all, she really shouldn't have kept them behind the bar so in a way was partly responsible for Mark's gross overreaction.

Clear brown eyes scrutinised her for what felt like for ever before a smile broke out on his face...

Her heart slammed. What a smile that was. It lit the whole of his face and, with that smile, Becky understood why Jenna and the thousands of other groupies were so infatuated with him.

'What are you doing the rest of the day?' he asked, stepping over to her and holding his arms out for his dog.

'Working...' Between them they got the dog from her arms into his, a feat not made easy as Emiliano was a good foot taller than her dinky size. She caught a wave of faded cologne mingled with fresh sweat and found her nostrils twitching for another sniff. 'Well, I was supposed to be working. I'm not sure if you firing Mark means I'm still fired or not.'

'I'll give you five hundred pounds if you'll look after the boys for me.'

'You what?'

He gave a lopsided grin. 'I've a final to play in three hours and I've just fired my dog-sitter.'

Two months later

Emiliano read the looping handwritten letter for a third time before scrunching it into his pocket and storming out of his English home. A phone call to the woman who'd just ruined his day went unanswered. Scowling at the heavy clouds overhead marring what should be a quintessential summer's day, he wasted thirty minutes searching for her, checking his world-class stables and the paddocks first.

As if he didn't have enough to contend with, what with the weekend at his Machiavellian mother's villa in Monte Cleure coming up and having to share air with his half-brother. He hadn't seen Damián since their father's funeral nearly six months ago. If he had his way, he'd never have to share air with him again, but this time tomorrow he'd be stuck in his rotten company.

When his phone rang he snatched it out of his pocket and scowled again to see his vet's name pop up on the screen rather than Becky's. Not even the excellent news that Matilde, a super-lative mare he'd had to retire from racing, was pregnant, could bring a smile to his face.

A figure walking over his pastureland in the distance caught his attention. Two smaller four-legged creatures bounding around it confirmed the figure to be Becky, and he marched briskly towards her.

His boys spotted him first and ran over for some fuss.

'What is the meaning of this?' he demanded when he reached her, waving the letter in her face.

She rolled her eyes and reached down to scoop up the dogs' ball with the launcher in her hand. 'My official resignation.'

'I do not accept it.'

She whipped the launcher through the air, sending the ball flying and the boys tearing off after it. Then she looked at Emiliano and shrugged. 'I'm leaving whether you accept it or not.'

'How can you do this to the boys? They adore you.'

'And I adore them, but when I took this job I told you it would only be temporary.'

'How am I supposed to find someone else at such short notice?'

She folded her arms across her considerable chest and gave him the look of patience mixed with exasperation he'd become so used to. 'Four weeks is hardly short notice, not when I told you two months ago I'd only be able to do the job for three months. I wrote the letter as a courtesy and a reminder for you to pull your finger out and find someone else. You've plenty of time to find a replacement.'

'I don't want a replacement.' In the two months she'd been their live-in sitter he hadn't had a moment's worry about his boys' care. 'I'll double your salary.'

Rufus had dropped the ball at her feet. She scooped it up and launched it again then flashed the smile that always made Emiliano's chest lighten and his loins throb.

At first glance, Becky was ordinary-looking. The day he'd met her she'd been wearing a uniform of black shirt and formless trousers, her ordinary long dark hair tied back, ordinary face free from make-up. Had his boys not found sanctuary and protection with her when they'd run away from Greta, their previous dog-sitter, he would never have looked twice at her. He'd already offered her the job as Greta's replacement when she'd smiled. And *pow*!

She dazzled. She was *beautiful*. Drop-dead gorgeous. Large green eyes, a snub nose and lips so wide and plump his mouth had yearned to feel if they were as soft as they looked. Days later, he'd seen her 'ordinary' hair loose and realised there was nothing ordinary about that either. A gleaming dark chestnut, it fell in thick waves halfway down her back. Added to the package was a friendly if occasionally fierce nature, a quick wit and a love of dogs that matched his own. If Becky Aldridge wasn't in his employ and therefore forbidden fruit he'd have bedded her in a heartbeat.

But she was in his employ and, if he had his way, would remain so.

'You're more than welcome to double it, starting now,' she said lightly, 'but I'm still leaving. I start my new job in six weeks.'

'Six weeks?' His outrage was immediate. 'Then why leave me in four?'

'Because I have things I need to sort before I start.'

Like a place to live. Becky had viewed rental properties online close to the laboratory she was soon to be working at and had set the ball rolling on one of them, but she still needed to buy furniture and get settled before she started the job.

'Tell them you've changed your mind.'

She smiled sympathetically. Poor Emiliano. Born into unimaginable wealth, he'd spent his life believing whatever he wanted he could have. Reality could be twisted to suit his needs. When she'd agreed to take the job he'd obviously decided to ignore the temporary bit and assumed he could charm her into staying.

'No.' She hadn't spent years working her brain to mush to throw it all away.

Before he could explode at her flat refusal, his phone rang. He glared as if it had personally offended him before answering.

While he chattered away in his native Argentine-Spanish, her resignation letter slipped from his hand. Clear brown eyes met hers and, with a malicious grin, he squished it with his boot.

She rolled her eyes. Having a four-month window before starting her research role at the end of September, Becky had sought a temporary job that kept her busy without being mentally taxing. Her brain needed a break. The hospitality role at the polo venue had fulfilled both criteria but she'd taken no joy from it, so when Emiliano had offered her the job as his live-in dog-sitter she'd jumped at the opportunity, accepting it on the strict understanding that it would only be until mid-September.

Becky had been raised with dogs and loved them. They were loyal in a way people never were and minding Emiliano's wonderful hounds certainly beat dealing with drunk humans. They were affectionate too, always wanting to cuddle up to her, something that never failed to make her heart swell. Working for Emiliano and living on his busy estate filled with no-nonsense horsey people had been a joy. He was the easiest person she'd ever worked for. In fairness, her job could hardly be called work, more paid fun, but as she'd learned during their first meeting, for all his good humour, you crossed him at your peril. Only a week ago, he'd unceremoniously fired one of his grooms for not meeting the high standard of care he required for his horses. He was equally ferocious on the polo field.

She'd finally got to grips with the game and

even started enjoying it. By always wearing her shades, no one could see her eyes following Emiliano's every move. It was never deliberate. There was something about the way he charged around the field on a horse—she would never understand why they insisted on calling them ponies—that captured her attention. Truth was, he captured her attention whatever he was doing. Truth was, even if she hadn't intended the job to be temporary from the start, she would still be resigning.

Long, lean and broad-shouldered, Emiliano's long face could have been crafted by Michelangelo. Wide, clear brown eyes, high cheekbones and a wide firm mouth counteracted a too-long nose. Topping it all was dark brown hair cut short at the sides and long at the top, which he rarely managed to tame. Becky quite understood why he set so many fully-grown women's pulses racing and it was becoming increasingly hard to keep her own pulse controlled around him or the jealousy that coiled inside her at the groupies who fawned over him wherever he went. A natural flirt, Emiliano had the ability to make any woman feel he only had eyes for her. Becky had to constantly remind herself that when he fixed those come-to-bed eyes on her and bestowed her with his lazy lopsided grin it wasn't anything special. Her reaction to it was nothing special either, as all the fawning groupies would testify.

It was the dreams that disturbed her most. Dreams from which she would wake flushed and throbbing. Meeting his eyes after one of those dreams was excruciating. Hiding her internal reaction to him was becoming harder by the day. The sooner she left the better. The sooner she started her new job and put her mind back to good use, the sooner she'd stop thinking of him and her life could return to normal.

His mood was much brighter when he ended the call. 'The Picasso they said was not for sale? It's mine,' he told her triumphantly.

'Congratulations.' As well as being one of the world's most successful horse breeders and a top polo player, Emiliano had a penchant for art and had opened galleries free to the general public in London, New York, Madrid and Buenos Aires filled with the exquisite work he'd acquired. 'If you open a gallery in Oxford you can display it there and I can visit when I have time off.'

'Oxford?'

'Didn't you read my résumé?' When he'd offered her the job, he'd told her to email her résumé to his PA for the staff files. She'd assumed basic curiosity about the woman he was entrusting his precious dogs to would compel him to read it.

He folded his arms across his chest and, face smug, said, 'I didn't need to. I'm an excellent judge of character.'

With another exaggerated roll of her eyes she shook her head and patted her thighs for the dogs' attention. The first drop of rain had landed on her nose and she wanted to get them inside before the heavens opened. 'You've got four weeks. I suggest you get recruiting.'

'I don't need to recruit,' he called as she strode away. 'You're staying.'

She turned back to face him and walked backwards. 'You're delusional.'

'Don't you know I always get what I want, *bomboncita*?'

'Then consider my leaving a much-needed favour to your ego.' Giving him one last cheeky wave, she turned back around and, dogs running alongside her, jogged back to the pretty cottage he'd given her as a perk of the job.

CHAPTER TWO

TRAVELLING BY PRIVATE jet was, Becky decided the next day, something everyone should experience once in their lives. Travelling by private jet with a grumpy billionaire, however, was something everyone should avoid. Not even Rufus and Barney had been able to put a smile on Emiliano's face.

She didn't have the faintest idea why a visit to his mother's villa should suck away his normal languid good humour and she didn't want to know. It was hard enough dealing with her physical response to him without adding personal issues to the mix, so she stuck her earphones in and closed her eyes. Even while she pretended to sleep for the duration of the flight she felt the tension emanating from him. When they landed and he stomped down the metal steps from his plane as if trying to smash through them, she bit her tongue to stop the questions clamouring on it forming. His bad moods, infrequent though they were, rarely lasted this long.

Swept from the airport by a gleaming black limousine, she had to peer through the tinted windows to see anything of Monte Cleure, a tiny principality wedged between France and Spain. From what she could see, it gleamed as brightly as the car.

It seemed as if no time had passed before they entered a rambling estate with breathtaking gardens. Becky peered again through the window, awestruck by the sprawling villa with its pale yellow walls and terracotta roof gleaming under cerulean skies rising before them like a squared-off horseshoe.

'We'll drop you and the boys at your lodging first,' Emiliano informed her. His jaw had set so tight she was surprised he could get any words out.

The driver came to a stop outside a one-storey lodge set in a thicket of woodland. One of a dozen identical staff lodges, it was painted the same colours as the main villa.

'Pretty,' she observed, only realising she'd spoken aloud when Emiliano's jaw loosened a touch.

'You should be comfortable here. Anything you're not happy with, let me know and I'll get it sorted.'

She ruffled Rufus's head and smiled. 'I'm sure we'll be fine.'

'You have the run of the estate to walk them.' As Emiliano's mother refused to allow his dogs in the villa, they would stay with Becky for the weekend. She didn't doubt Emiliano would drop in to visit them and whisk them away at every opportunity. 'Carry your passport with you—there's an army of security guards patrolling the land.'

'Are they armed?'

'*Sí.*'

The driver opened her door. 'I'll try not to get shot then,' she quipped.

She caught a glimpse of white teeth before she swung her legs out of the car. The dogs jumped out after her and waited as she said goodbye to their master.

Emiliano saluted. '*Chau, bomboncita.*'

'*Hasta luego,*' she replied. See you later. Usually when she said one of the Argentine-Spanish terms she'd picked up from him he grinned. This time his smile was more of a grimace.

She watched him be driven away, wondering again why a visit to his mother should put him in such a bad temper.

Emiliano greeted the merry widow, his mother Celeste, with the air-kisses they'd used since he was a boy.

'No lady-friend with you?' she asked, tucking her arm into his elbow as they strolled the villa's grounds.

For some reason his mind immediately flew to his English dog-sitter. 'Not this time.'

'That's not like you, *mijito*. I always look forward to seeing which ravishing creature you'll have on your arm for my party. My guests do too.'

Celeste's annual summer party. The reason he was there.

'I've been too busy to date,' he lied. Truth was, he hadn't been on a date in two months. The women who swarmed around him like wasps around an open jam jar had lost their appeal. He had no idea why.

'Thinking ahead to when you take over the Delgado Group?'

'Pointless considering Father's will might

still turn up.' Eduardo, his adoptive father, had died nearly six months ago. The day of his funeral, Emiliano's half-brother Damián had discovered the will missing from their father's safe. Emiliano didn't need to communicate verbally with him to know Damián thought him responsible for it, and for the missing document that had signed the Delgado Group into Damián's sole control. If they weren't found within the next three weeks then, under Monte Cleure's archaic law, the eldest son inherited everything. Which meant Emiliano would inherit the multibillion-dollar finance business Damián had been promised and, if Emiliano was feeling charitable, had earned the right to inherit.

'It might,' she conceded. 'But if it doesn't your father's empire falls to you.'

He tightened his lips to stop them saying, *He wasn't my father.* His real father had been an Argentine polo player who'd died when Emiliano had been ten weeks old. A year later, Celeste had married Eduardo, who'd adopted her baby son and given him his name but never his love or approval. Emiliano's only usefulness had been as proof of Celeste's fertility.

Eduardo had needed an heir for the business. He'd found that in Damián.

The irony that the unwanted non-blood spawn might inherit Eduardo's entire estate was almost funny. The months Emiliano had spent working for the Delgado Group a decade ago had ended in disaster and acrimony. Having zero interest in finance, he'd only taken the job for Celeste. It had been the last thing he'd ever done or would ever do for her. As a child he'd worshipped the ground she walked on. And then he'd woken up to who she was. A narcissistic bitch.

But she was still his mother, his flesh and blood. She was a hard woman to feel any kind of affection for but he supposed he felt something akin to love for her.

'I don't want it,' he said.

'Then what will you do? Give it to Damián?' she added with a tinkle of laughter.

Emiliano smiled grimly. Where his relationship with Celeste was complicated, his relationship with Damián was simple—they loathed each other. They might not have exchanged a word in a decade but they had to suffer each other's company twice a year. It had always given him perverse pleasure to bring a scantily dressed woman with him to the annual summer party. Seeing Damián's serious face pucker with disapproval was a never ceasing joy. Damián, like his father, had always thought the worst of Emiliano. Proving them right was something that never grew old.

'I don't know what I'll do.' Burn it to the ground? That was one possibility.

'I appreciate your life is full with the running of your stables…' she made it sound as if he had a couple of small paddocks he kept his horses in rather than world-class stables strategically located around the world in which he bred and trained horses for racing, polo and dressage competitions '…and the polo team and that you would be reluctant to step back from it. I have invaluable experience with all aspects of the Delgado Group. If you feel running it would be too much for you, I am willing to step in and run it. On your behalf, of course.'

'Of course.' He hid a knowing smile. He'd been waiting for this conversation. Celeste was power-hungry in all aspects of life. It wouldn't surprise him in the least if it came out that she'd been the one to steal Eduardo's will and business document. If they were found, any influence Celeste had on the business would be gone. Damián would want to keep control for himself. 'But this is a conversation for another time. When's Damián due?'

'His jet's just landed, so not long. He's brought a lady friend.'

'So you said. Must be serious.' Damián hadn't introduced a woman to the family in, oh, it must be fifteen years. He was probably scared Celeste would frighten them off.

Celeste arched her brows. 'Be nice to her.'

He grunted. His beef was with his brother and no one else. 'I'm going to freshen up. I'll see you at lunch.'

'We'll eat outside. You are *not* to bring those mutts.'

He answered with a grin and strolled back into the villa he'd spent much of his childhood in. His mother's insistence that he not bring his dogs to lunch was too great a challenge to resist.

•

Emiliano straightened his bow tie with a grimace. He loathed wearing suits of any kind but DJs were the worst. Usually he enjoyed

Celeste's summer parties. The guest list was always inspired, hundreds of the rich, famous and eccentric letting their hair down and behaving disgracefully, staggering to their waiting cars and helicopters clutching their lavish goody bags.

However, there had been little enjoyment to be found so far that weekend, and he didn't see why the party should be any different. On the surface, things were exactly as they always were when the family came together: Celeste acting the role of High Priestess, Damián brooding, Emiliano finding amusement in his discomfort, the two brothers ignoring each other in a deliberate manner and making no effort to hide their mutual loathing. But the tension that was always there when they came together felt different this time. Suspicion and distrust underlined every movement and left him with an acrid taste on his tongue.

On impulse, he pulled his phone out and called Becky. She answered after three rings.

'Where are you?' he asked.

'Walking the boys and trying not to get shot by your mum's security guards.'

He grinned. He could always trust Becky

to put a smile on his face. 'Will you be back soon?'

'I doubt it. We're about two miles away in the forest. Why? Is everything okay?'

No, everything was not okay. There was a feeling of dread in his stomach much like he'd experienced as a child in the days before his school reports had been sent out.

'*Si*. Just thought I'd visit the boys before I start behaving disgracefully and shaming my family.'

Her laughter echoed like music in his ears. 'I imagine we'll be back in half an hour.'

'Don't worry about it. I'll see you...them... in the morning. Have a nice evening.'

'And you. Enjoy the party.'

'I'll try.'

He put his phone in his pocket and drank a measure of the Scotch he'd poured himself. As he sloshed it round his mouth, he imagined Becky at his side, dressed to the nines. He'd never actually seen her in a dress. Or a skirt. He'd never even seen her legs; as she was always out with the dogs over fields and woodland, she wore jeans to protect them. She had the most fabulous hourglass figure though, a real buxom beauty with killer curves and her bottom *filled* those jeans.

Those same musings ran through his head as the guests arrived and he noticed that hardly any of the female guests had curves of any kind, and those that did had gained them with the help of an able surgeon. While hardly anyone had an ounce of spare fat on them, there was, he estimated, enough filler pumped into all the beautiful faces to fill a swimming pool. Becky, he was quite certain, would soon find laughter lines appearing around her eyes and mouth. He was equally certain that she wouldn't go the filler route. If he had his way, she would still be in his life—his *dogs'* life— long enough for him to find out personally.

As soon as this weekend was done, he would get straight onto the important task of convincing Becky to stay. His boys meant the world to him, and the peace of mind her care and attention for them gave was worth whatever it took to make her stay. She pretended not to care about money but everyone had a price. She must be holding out for something. Why throw in the towel on a job that paid well and had unlimited perks for a limited role in hospitality otherwise?

'Emiliano!' The shriek of his name pierced straight through him and, wincing, he turned to find Kylie, a spoilt English heiress, tottering over to him in heels so high they could be reclassified as stilts. A moment later and a pair of bony arms were thrown around his neck and his airways filled with a perfume so sweet and cloying he almost gagged.

'You are *so* naughty,' she pouted. 'You said you would call me.'

He grinned sheepishly and unlocked her wrists from around his neck. 'My apologies. Life has been hectic.'

Kylie had been at the polo competition when his dogs had briefly gone missing. She'd joined his team when they'd celebrated their semifinal win. He vaguely remembered promising to take her out for dinner once the competition was done with and then promptly forgot all about her.

Why was that? he puzzled. Kylie was exactly his type—beautiful, blonde and long-legged and with only a few brain cells rattling around in her head. Emiliano's one serious relationship a decade ago had been with a woman blessed with ferocious natural intelligence. It was his misfortune that she'd also been blessed with natural deviousness and criminality, something he'd discovered far too late and which had seen his world collapse around him.

As Kylie continued to chatter, his brother came into his eyeline.

What was going on with him? Something was up; he sensed it deep inside him. And what was he doing with a woman like Mia? The Brit Damián had brought with him to the party had joined the family for lunch the previous day and gone to the casino with them in the evening, and had immediately proved herself to be fun. The last woman Damián had introduced the family to had been as much fun as a Benedictine monk on a stag weekend. Emiliano sensed a dark undertone beneath his half-brother and his new lover's sociable smiles. It only increased the sense of doom that had been building since his arrival in Monte Cleure.

Something was going to happen. Something bad. He could feel it in his bones.

* * *

Becky was so deep in sleep that it took the dogs barking to rouse her to the banging on her front door.

Stumbling out of bed, she shrugged herself into her robe and padded out of the room, trying not to trip over the dogs.

'I'm coming!' she shouted at the unceasing banging, knowing perfectly well it was Emiliano, probably drunk and wanting to see the boys. He'd often turned up at the cottage he'd given her on his English estate after a night out just to see his dogs.

She unlocked the door and yanked it open but her prepared stern words died on her tongue when she saw his haggard face.

'What's wrong?' she asked, stepping aside to let him in.

He staggered to her small living room without answering or putting the light on, and slumped onto the sofa. He barely lifted a hand to pat his beloved dogs' heads.

'Emiliano?'

Haunted eyes met hers but he didn't speak.

Crouching next to him, she took his hand in hers. It was icy cold. She patted his arm. His dinner jacket was damp. She caught a whiff of chlorine. Had he been swimming in his clothes? And then she noticed the red marks blazing over his knuckles. Had Emiliano been *fighting*?

Her chest tightened unbearably. Something was wrong. Dreadfully wrong.

'Use the shower,' she urged. 'You need to get warm.'

He closed his eyes and rested his head back. His chest rose sharply, his features so tight she feared they could snap.

She patted his icy hand again and wished she could put it to her mouth and blow warmth onto it as her mother had done on winter days when Becky had been a little girl and her mother had been a real mother to her. 'I'll make you a hot drink.'

In the kitchen she put the kettle on and dug out the hot chocolate she'd spotted earlier in a cupboard. The rotors of a helicopter sounded above the lodging. Not even midnight and guests were leaving? What the heck had happened?

The living room was empty when she returned with his drink but, before she could worry, she heard the shower going. Then it occurred to her—he had nothing to change into. And she had nothing that would fit him.

Inspiration struck and she shrugged her towelling robe off. She knocked on the bathroom door and shouted that she was leaving it by the door for him.

She tried to keep the dogs calm while she waited for Emiliano to finish in the bathroom. Rufus and Barney had picked up on their master's mood and seemed unable to settle. She didn't have to wait long. Her heart tore to see his long, lean frame clad in her blue cotton robe. On Becky, it came to mid-calf. On Emiliano, it came to mid-thigh. On anyone else it would look ridiculous. It only made him sexier and she had to drag her eyes away from the deeply tanned, ridiculously muscular legs and snatch a deep inhalation to counter the rapid beat of her heart.

He hovered in the doorway. 'Can I sleep here tonight?' The drawling voice that normally vibrated with life was monotone.

If she hadn't already guessed something bad had happened, this would have clinched it. Even the night he'd taken his polo team out to celebrate another cup win and knocked on her door at two in the morning more than a little inebriated, he hadn't asked to stay or even hinted at it. He'd accepted a black coffee then staggered back to his mansion with the dogs at his heels.

'Sure... I'll make the spare bed up.'

'I just need to get my head down for a few hours.'

'Stay as long as you like. I'll find some bedding for you. Your drink's on the table.'

He met her stare briefly and nodded.

The staff lodge she'd been given had two bedrooms but only one of the beds had been prepared. She found spare sheets in the airing cupboard. It wasn't much, just a couple of cotton blankets, but the summer evening was warm. Unable to find a pillow, she took one from her own bed and carried the bundle to the spare room. She made the bed then returned to the living room, where she found him looking out of the window, his drink in hand.

'The spare bed's made for you,' she said softly. 'I'm going back to bed. Are you going to be okay?'

He turned to look at her and blinked as if

waking from sleep, then raised his mug in a half-hearted salute.

Her heart ached at his wretchedness. Her arms ached to wrap around him and give comfort. Her brain ached at all the possibilities of what could have caused such devastation. 'Get some sleep,' she whispered.

She felt his eyes follow her as she left the living room and headed back to bed.

Lying there in the darkness, she wondered how she could have slept through the noise of the helicopters considering the racket they continued to make. She hoped they weren't too noisy to stop Emiliano from sleeping.

When she finally fell asleep, thoughts of Emiliano were the last thoughts in her head. Just as they'd been every night since the day she'd met him.

She slept deeply until loud, haunted shouts woke her in an instant.

CHAPTER THREE

A HAND TOUCHED his head. 'Emiliano, wake up.'

Emiliano opened his eyes with a start. His body was racked with tremors, flesh riddled with goose bumps, his insides feeling as if they'd turned into a mass block of ice. Perched tentatively on the edge of the bed, a hazy shadow in the darkness of the small room, was Becky.

He grabbed at his hair and tried to catch a breath.

He hadn't had a nightmare like that since he was a small child. He was living a nightmare. The wicked witch of childhood stories. His own mother. A killer.

She covered his hand and flinched. 'You're still freezing.'

He swallowed hard. The enveloping coldness had made his throat close.

'I'll get my duvet,' she whispered. Rising to

her feet, she slipped out of the room, leaving him alone in the still darkness. He tightened the sheets around him but couldn't stop shivering. Didn't dare close his eyes. He didn't think he could endure the dreams that came with sleep. He was so damn cold his teeth chattered.

Becky returned in moments and draped the duvet over him before gently telling him to move over. The single bed hardly dipped as she slipped under the bedding and wrapped her arms around him.

She held him tightly, tenderly, rubbing her warm hands over his back and arms, her face pressed against his chest, the warmth of her breath gently heating his skin. He rested his cheek into the top of her head and held her just as tightly. The soft scent of her shampoo and silkiness of her hair played into his senses, soothing him.

Slowly, under Becky's tender embrace, his frozen body defrosted. The fog that had stupefied his brain began to clear.

He remembered trying hard to get in the party spirit, even throwing himself fully dressed in the swimming pool and horsing around. He remembered climbing the stairs, intending to change his sodden clothing but finding his brother outside his quarters. He remembered the damning evidence Damián had shown him against their mother, remembered the piercing agony when Damián had asked about his own involvement in the heinous act, the throbbing in his knuckles from when he'd punched a wall a reminder of how close they'd come to physical blows. And he remembered them pulling together as brothers for the first time in their lives to confront their evil, Machiavellian mother.

He remembered needing to escape the villa. Along with his brother, he'd detonated a bomb in the middle of the party but by then had been too numb to care about the wreckage.

But he barely remembered walking to the lodge. His aimless escape had taken him to Becky.

Her warming hands had reached the base of his spine when they suddenly jerked away. 'Are you naked?'

'Sorry,' he muttered, cursing himself. Until that moment, his nakedness hadn't even registered in his own head. He hadn't been aware, either, that his body had roused itself to the beautiful woman he'd curled into.

'It's okay…' Becky, who'd shifted sharply at the shock of heat that had torn through her at the realisation of his nudity, tried to breathe. Everything inside her had tautened like stretched nerves.

The foolhardiness of getting under the covers with this hunk of a man hadn't entered her head. A deep-rooted need to warm his freezing body and soothe him from the nightmare that had tormented him had overridden everything. Now she found herself sharing a single bed with a naked man but, instead of freezing in fear, she found her hands aching to touch the muscular smoothness again and repeatedly having to swallow back moisture and breathe through her nose because the musky scent of his skin was setting off crazy things inside her. The greater her awareness of the crazy reactions, the more she became aware of others, of the tight heat bubbling low inside her, the new, strange excitement thickening and building, the strange sensitivity of her skin, the tingling sensation of her breasts pressed against his chest…

'Sorry,' he repeated, speaking into the top of her head before rolling onto his back.

Still trying to breathe, she rolled onto her back too and shuffled up so her head was on the pillow…but that brought no succour as the bed was so small the sides of their bodies remained pressed together. Their heads were so close the strands of his hair brushed against her forehead.

If it wasn't obvious that something terrible had happened to him, she would go back to her own bed, use towels and anything else she could find as bedding. But she didn't want to leave him, not in this state. She could still hear the shouts of his nightmare in her ears.

By unspoken agreement they moved in unison and turned their backs to each other. Becky pulled the duvet over her shoulders and closed her eyes. Their bodies no longer touched but there could only be millimetres between them and her skin quivered with awareness. Her heart thrashed with such intensity the beats resounded in her head. How long they lay there, unmoving, barely a breath escaping their mouths, she didn't know. If the tension crackling between them had a colour it would be scorching red.

She fought her body, forcing it to lie like a statue, terrified to risk their skin brushing, terrified of unleashing the burn building inside her.

As deeply attracted to him as she was, Becky didn't want to be one of Emiliano's bedpost notches. No sane woman would. She didn't want to be another faceless woman on a list so long it should be called a scroll. The danger of her response to him had been apparent from the start and she'd imposed a friendly distance between them and sensed he'd imposed one too, an invisible line neither of them breached.

That line had been severed.

She couldn't breathe. Her quivering skin felt as if it had come to life. Never had she had such awareness of the mechanics of her body: her heart pumping so violently, the weight of her tingling breasts, the melting of her pelvis...

Emiliano tried to sleep. He'd turned his back to Becky and closed his eyes. The nightmare that had called her to him had dissolved, not even fragments remaining. Everything that had happened that night had been driven out, his senses attuned only to the woman lying so close to him.

Grimly, he told himself to stay exactly where he was and not move.

How the hell had he found himself in bed naked with Becky?

He did not involve himself with employees. He didn't care how sexy they were or how heavily they flirted with him and batted their lashes, he kept his hands off. Becky had been the biggest test of that resolve since he'd made it ten years ago, and she'd never given him so much as a suggestive smile. Seeing her every day in those tight jeans that caressed her fabulous curves would test even the holiest man's resolve, especially when she bent over to scoop a ball up, and then there was the way her breasts bounced when she threw the ball... *Dios*, it was enough to make a man salivate.

And now he was naked in bed with her and the desire he'd kept under the tightest of leashes was pulling madly for release. Every inch of his body throbbed with awareness, heart beating weightily against his ribs, loins burning. A lock of her long hair lay against his back, the strands feeling like tickling silk against his skin.

Dios, this was torture.

He had to leave. Right now. Put his damp clothes back on and take his boys to the villa. They could run riot over the polished floors to their hearts' content.

Gritting his teeth, he sat up and threw the duvet off him. 'I have to go.'

A needle tip of panic pressed into Becky's chest and, before she knew what she was doing, she had pushed herself upright.

Though it was dark, her eyes were adjusted enough to see the rigidity of Emiliano's muscular back, and she clutched tightly to the duvet to stop her hand placing itself flat on it.

Let him go. Lie back down and go to sleep.

But the burn spreading like a wave from deep in her pelvis told her sleep was impossibly far away. For the first time in her life she was caught in desire's claw, the fight she'd been waging with herself liquefying.

Over the thudding of her heart, she heard him take a deep inhalation. Then another.

She inched closer to him without any thought. 'Emiliano?'

Slowly, his head turned.

The thudding of her heart became a thunderous canter.

Never had she seen his features so tight, the nostrils flare so rapidly. Or the expression in his eyes, which held hers so starkly.

The taut stillness stretched for an age before something that looked like pain contorted his face and in the whisper of a moment his body twisted and he lunged, hands cupping her face tightly as he crushed his mouth to hers.

Taken off-guard, Becky had no time to mount a defence. Heat ignited inside her like a furnace and she leaned into the kiss with a moan of relief. Her lips parted and then they were moving ferociously in time with his, her senses engulfed with the taste of something so hot and intoxicating that any defence she could have mounted would have melted instantly.

In what could only have been seconds, she was flat on her back below Emiliano's lean, muscular body. There was a moment of stillness as she gazed into his pulsing eyes before their mouths fused back together in a kiss so hard and deep it erased any coherent thought.

For the first time in her life she didn't want

to think. She wanted to feel. She wanted to feel…everything.

Her suddenly greedy hands ran through Emiliano's hair and over his neck, fingers touching and exploring every part she could reach, his hands sweeping over her sides with the same urgency. Her cotton T-shirt was pulled over her head and then her naked breasts were pressed against his hard chest, right until he dived a hand between them and spread his fingers over the sensitised flesh, making her gasp at the pleasure this induced and Emiliano groan and mutter something unintelligible. His groan deepened when he slipped his hand into her shorts and touched her where no man had touched before.

The furnace in her grew with every kiss and touch, melting every part until she was nothing but molten liquid. There was a deep ache low inside her, the pulsations she'd often experienced at unbidden times when her fantasises about this man had pushed their way into her mind before she could stop them magnified. Every time his erection brushed against her thigh the pulsations turned into a strong spasm of need and she pressed herself even closer, her body taking the lead over a mind that had become lost in a drugged, sensitised fog called Emiliano.

Together, they pulled her cotton shorts off and then she was as naked as he and too drunk on the wonderful sensations rippling through her to care. Nothing mattered, only *this*, this hunger, this unquenchable fire.

Her legs parted instinctively as their tongues entwined in a heady dance of their own making, and then he was right where she craved him to be until, with one long thrust, he was buried deep inside her and she cried out the last of the air she had left in her lungs. If there was pain, she didn't notice. Emiliano was inside her, filling her, and it felt incredible. From the strangled groan that fell from his mouth into hers, the pleasure was shared.

Legs wrapped tightly around him, hands gripped together, Becky closed her eyes and submitted herself entirely to the intensity of his lovemaking.

In and out he thrust, his groin grinding against hers, driving the fever in her blood to boiling point. She responded by instinct, letting her body guide her, the pulsations inside her growing and growing, reaching, searching for *something*...

Something shattered inside her. Something that set off a riptide of unimaginable pleasure pulsing like a runaway train through her blood, her bones, her flesh, so powerful her back arched and a feral moan ripped from her throat.

The mutters in her ear from Emiliano's tongue had become a distant echo as she clung tightly to him while she rode the waves, but there was a dim awareness of his changing of tempo. His thrusts became harder and more urgent, and then her name flew from his mouth before he cried out and thrust so hard into her and for so long that their bodies fused together to become one.

The first thing that really penetrated Emiliano's brain was the strength of his heart. He'd never known it beat so hard or so fast. The second awareness was the strength of Becky's heartbeat crashing through their conjoined skin in time with his own and the raggedness of her breaths perfectly matching his. The third was that he was still burrowed deep inside her.

The earthy scent of their lovemaking filled his senses. His loins still twitched at the strength of his climax…

And that was when sanity came crashing down and he pulled away from her so quickly he created a draught.

Swinging his legs over the side of the bed, he grabbed at his hair, curses flying from his tongue in all the languages he knew.

'That was not supposed to happen,' he said between gulps of air.

The woman he'd just made love to didn't answer.

Dios, he couldn't bring himself to look at her. What the hell had he just done? Of all the stupid, idiotic, *foolish* things…

He should have left while he'd had the chance.

What the hell had compelled him to come to her in the first place? Had he been subconsciously seeking his boys? But that only then begged the question of why he hadn't collected them and gone back to the villa. It wasn't as if he was going to see his mother; she'd escaped on a friend's helicopter.

Self-recriminating rage and nausea roiled violently in his stomach. What the hell had he *done*?

'Tell me you're on the pill?' he demanded as he scraped his fingers over his skull.

Her continued silence gave him the answer and sent his roiling stomach dropping to his feet.

Never in his life had he failed to use contraception.

Never had he lost control as he'd just done with Becky.

And never had he hated himself as much as he did right then.

Damn it all to *hell*.

'Where are you in your cycle?' He knew his tone was too rough, that he was behaving deplorably, but he was helpless to stop. He'd stepped into quicksand and was fighting to stop himself being swallowed up.

He sensed her flinch as she sat up.

'I think you need to leave.' Becky's words were delivered with a curtness he'd never thought to hear from lips that were even softer to the touch than he'd imagined. Sweet and plump like a marshmallow. A temptation too far, even for him.

'Don't worry, I'm going. Just tell me how worried we need to be first.'

Becky stared at the muscular back, as rigid as it had been before his whole demeanour had changed and passion had overtaken them both, and wanted to curl into a ball and sob her eyes out.

In the space of minutes she'd gone from feeling as if she'd learned to fly to feeling as if she'd been dropped in the gutter. What had been the most incredible experience of her life had been ruined. Emiliano's cruel belligerence made her want to scrub her skin clean.

If she'd ever thought about how it would be to face him straight after she would have expected bawdy humour before a subtle extraction from her bed, no promises but no recriminations either. Possibly a fleeting kiss and a wink before he said a nonchalant goodbye.

But she hadn't faced him yet. The coward was still to look at her.

'*You* have nothing to worry about,' she said, snatching up her discarded T-shirt.

'Don't play games,' he snarled. 'If my failure to use a condom results in a baby then it *is* my problem. How worried do I need to be?'

Becky would have laughed if she didn't feel so much like weeping. Her menstrual cycle had always been as regular as clockwork. She was exactly mid-cycle, the time of the month when signs of her fertility made themselves known. Tender breasts, a slight rise of body temperature...

Maybe that was why she'd been so receptive to Emiliano, she thought with only a minuscule amount of hope. It hadn't been *him* so much, more a primal part of her acting as nature had designed.

'Very.' Shrugging the T-shirt over her head, she pushed the duvet off, jumped out of bed and headed for the door. 'I'm going to take a shower. See yourself out.'

His head turned. There was one moment of eye contact, moment enough to make her heart leap into her throat, before she left the room, only to find his damp clothes in a heap on the bathroom floor. Holding her breath, she scooped them into her arms and flung them into the corridor, then locked the door.

Shaking, she stripped her T-shirt off but avoided looking at the mirror. She couldn't bear to see her reflection.

Emiliano felt as if he'd been punched by a heavyweight with guilt. All he wanted was to crawl into his bed and sleep for a year. When he woke, he wanted this whole day to have been a nightmare he could shake off and forget about.

Becky must have turned the hallway light on for he suddenly became aware of illumination pooling into the room.

Unsteadily, he got to his feet. It suddenly seemed imperative that he be gone before she finished in the shower. He vaguely remembered leaving his clothes in the bathroom. If necessary, he would walk back to the villa wrapped in the bedsheets.

About to leave the room, he abruptly stopped and cast his gaze around it one last time...

What was that on the bedsheet?

Rubbing his hand over his mouth, he approached it cautiously, as if it were something that could leap off and sink its venomous teeth into his neck.

When he saw what it was, comprehension of what it meant hit him and the world began to spin.

He wished it *had* been something venomous.

On the bedsheet was a smear of blood.

CHAPTER FOUR

BECKY WAS ON her third coffee, her bags packed for the return journey to England, when a sharp rap on the front door announced Emiliano's arrival.

She'd packed those bags debating whether to just run. Leave. Find someone to whisk her to the airport and never look back. Anything but face him in the cold light of day.

But to run would be too much like what her father had done when the divorce had been finalised a year ago. The way she felt towards both her parents meant she would never do anything from either of their playbooks. More than that, she couldn't leave without saying goodbye to Rufus and Barney or leave Emiliano without care for them.

She needed to front this out. Only for another four weeks…no, three and a half weeks.

Heart lurching painfully, she pinched the

bridge of her nose and took a deep breath before rising from the sofa to open it.

He stood at the doorway, stubble covering his jawline, eyes puffy, hair damp, casually dressed in black jeans and a white T-shirt that perfectly accentuated his gorgeous frame.

How she kept her features from crumpling she didn't know. Memories of that lean frame naked and entwined with hers flew through her, not in pictures—it had been too dark for her to see him in anything but shadows—but as sensation.

Damn her heart for beating so madly to see him.

Damn her pulses for surging to meet his eye.

And damn him for still making her senses swirl despite looking as if he hadn't slept a wink since leaving her bed six hours ago. Becky hadn't slept either and knew it showed on her face too.

The awkwardness of their first contact was eased by Rufus and Barney bounding straight inside, tails wagging happily, the pair oblivious to the tension between their two favourite humans.

Wordlessly, she stepped aside to let him in.

'Leaving already, are we?' she asked dully.

'No.' He rammed his hands in his pockets. 'We need to stay a few more days. Maybe a week.'

She shrugged. She wouldn't ask why.

He nodded at the coffee pot. 'May I?'

She shrugged again. 'Help yourself.'

Picking up her own coffee cup from the counter, she opened the French windows and stepped into the empty staff garden. It was easier to breathe in the fresh air, safe from Emiliano's freshly showered scent.

He followed a minute later, joining her at the outdoor table, the dogs racing outside with him. It was only nine a.m. and already the sky was a brilliant blue, the warmth of the sun falling gently onto them. In a few hours it would be hot enough to burn.

'About last night...' he began.

She cut him off. 'I don't want to talk about it. It happened. It won't happen again.'

If she could, she would pretend it had never happened. But that wouldn't happen until her skin stopped tingling. She could still feel the marks where his fingers had caressed her. She was having to fight her eyes from meeting his, terrified of the feelings that ruptured through her whenever she got caught in his gaze, terrified of the feelings erupting inside her at his closeness.

Jaw tight, he inclined his head. 'We might have made a life.'

Her stomach dived. This was the one thing she'd refused to think about since he'd gone but his words opened the floodgates she'd suppressed and almost made her double over with fear.

Nature wouldn't be so cruel, would it? She remembered a boy from school solemnly informing all the girls in their form that you couldn't get pregnant if you did 'it' standing up or if it was your first time. She'd asked her mum, who'd still been a loving mum back then, who'd smiled widely and shaken her head. 'Honey,' she'd said, 'don't believe anything a man tells you when it comes to contraception. Take charge of it for yourself.'

To remember that tenderness from the woman who'd so recently cut her out of her life was like prodding an open wound, but Becky had taken those nearly ten-years-old words of wisdom to heart. She'd believed that when she met the man she could build a relationship with they would take things slowly. She'd thought her first time would come after careful consideration and planning. She'd believed she would have time to protect herself.

And now she had to hope and pray that, despite everything she'd spent years learning about the human body, the boy from her form had been right. She needed all the divine intervention she could get.

Swallowing back the metallic taste in her throat, she said, 'If you're a man who believes in prayers, I suggest you put your hands together.'

He muttered something she didn't need to be a linguist to understand was a curse.

Time stretched in silence before he said, 'I'm sorry, *bomboncita*.'

She gritted her teeth against the surge of warmth that filled her. She'd always secretly liked it when he called her that. But that was before. Now, in the after, being called the name he must have called hundreds of women before her was just another reminder of Emiliano's womanising ways and her own utter stupidity.

'Don't call me that. And I don't want your apologies. We were both there.'

'The way I spoke to you after...' He breathed in heavily. 'I was out of order.'

Oh, God, she was going to cry. 'Agreed.'

'*Bom*... Becky, what happened...'

'I don't want to talk about it.' She blinked rapidly, doing her darnedest to stop the tears from spilling. 'It's history. I've already put it from my mind so I suggest you forget it too. If a baby's been made then we'll deal with it but, until that happens, I would thank you to never speak of it again.'

'Were you a virgin?'

Mortification thrashed through her and she shoved her chair back violently and got to her feet. 'I *said* I don't want to talk about it.'

His face only became grimmer. 'Answer my question first.'

'What difference does it make? None at all.'

He banged his fist on the table, features twisting with anger. 'Of course it makes a difference!'

'Why?' She threw her arms in the air and tried her hardest to keep a lid on the emotions crashing through her, so many of them: fear, anger, humiliation, despair and, worse than all that, awareness. For him. An awareness so strong that, should he touch her, she feared she would melt into him before she had the sense to smack him away. She'd guessed that making love changed a person but not like *this*. Whatever happened with the baby situation, Becky knew their night together had changed something in her, but for Emiliano...

She didn't doubt that within weeks of her leaving his employ he'd struggle to remember her name.

'Are you going to fake some chivalry?' she demanded, her voice rising to match the rising anguish and panic. 'Why should me being a virgin make any difference when it's never made a difference to your treatment of women before? You love 'em and leave 'em regardless.'

His anger finally reaching tipping point, Emiliano jumped to his feet. Since leaving Becky's bed he hadn't slept a jot, the memories of their explosive lovemaking so strong that they vied with the despair his mother's actions had evoked. But it was the evidence of Becky's virginity casting the darkest cloud.

Had he hurt her? The mere thought sliced his

heart. It hadn't crossed his mind for a second that she could be a virgin. She was twenty-five years old! She should have had many lovers by now. If he could turn back time and stop himself from knocking on her door, he would do it in a heartbeat.

And if he could turn off the awareness still thrumming wildly in his blood and loins for her...

Dios, every inch of him ached to taste those plump lips again, then taste all the parts he hadn't tasted in the explosion of passion that had taken them in its grip.

'I might not be a saint but I've never treated women in the way you've just implied.'

'You *liar*. You have no respect for women. We're just a commodity to you, something to use when you're in the mood and then discarded the next day.'

Something sharp stabbed his chest at this exquisitely delivered observation but he pushed it to one side. His past lovers had always known the score. He'd never lied to them. The only woman he'd slept with in the past decade without making the score clear beforehand was the woman who stood before him now, as many emotions blazing from her green eyes as he had curdling in his guts.

'If that was true then tell me what the hell I'm doing here right now.'

'Scared that your recklessness might have made a baby!'

'*My* recklessness?'

'You started it!'

'And you, *bomboncita*, were a *very* willing participant...' so willing his loins tightened to remember her breathless moans and the passion of her kisses '...so don't try and twist this mess onto me. It was a mistake that you've already admitted we were both party to, so stop with the blame game and take some responsibility for your own actions.'

'If I'm pregnant then it's a responsibility I'll bear for the rest of my life.'

'And my life too.'

'Oh, are you going to carry it and give birth to it and give up all your dreams for it?' Her laughter had a strong tinge of hysteria. 'The most you'll have to do is chuck some money at it and then carry on sleeping your way around the world as if nothing's changed.'

'We don't even know if you've conceived

and already you've decided what my future actions will be? Your opinion of me is worse than I believed.'

'If you didn't want a reputation as a playboy you should have been choosier about who you shared a bed with!'

'I didn't hear any complaints last night,' he said pointedly, stepping closer to her as if her body had a magnetic charge his responded to.

'There wasn't time,' she retorted, the heat in her voice matched by the heat flushing over her cheeks.

'Is that the voice of experience talking?' he taunted. 'How about a repeat performance so you can judge accordingly?'

Green eyes pulsed as her chin jutted defiantly. 'If your first performance is the standard then I'll pass.'

'And you call *me* a liar?' Snaking an arm around her waist, he pulled her flush to him and fused his mouth to hers. Her response was as immediate as it had been the night before, arms looping tightly around his neck, kissing him back with the same rabid hunger that controlled him.

Dios, she tasted so damn headily sweet, even

more than he remembered, and when he gripped her delicious bottom to press her even more tightly against him, and she felt his excitement through the denim jeans they both wore, her moan only made him harder.

Pressing her against the table for support, he slipped a hand up her T-shirt and groaned into her mouth, feeling the silky softness of her skin, his groan deepening when he reached the underside of her breasts, frustratingly enclosed by a lacy bra.

There had been no time for him to even look at her naked when they'd made love. The need to be inside her had been too strong, too consuming, a need he'd never felt before. Virgin or not, Becky's response had been every bit as fevered. She'd wanted it as much as he and, for all her taunts, her response right then was proof that fever still lived in her blood as much as it lived in his. Her thighs parted and a hand dived inside the collar of his T-shirt, nails scratching against his feverish skin.

Later, he would wonder how far they would have taken it in the staff garden if Rufus hadn't decided that whatever the humans were doing looked like something fun he needed to join in with, and leapt at them.

In an instant, they pulled apart.

Becky scrambled to straighten her T-shirt but her hands were shaking so hard it took several attempts to get hold of the fabric then sink onto a chair, her boneless limbs struggling to support her weight.

Too mortified to look at him, she covered her face and fought to get air into her lungs. She wished the ground would swallow her up. Bad enough she'd melted into a puddle for him in the dark of night but to do the same in broad daylight when any of the live-in villa staff could be watching them…? Had she lost all her good sense and modesty along with her virginity?

She heard Emiliano sit heavily on the seat beside her. 'Becky…'

'Just go,' she whispered from behind her trembling hands. 'And please, find a replacement for me. Do it now. I'll stay until you find someone or until my notice has been worked, and I'll care for the boys as I always do but any communication about them can be done by phone. I don't want to see you or speak to you unless it's absolutely necessary.'

She heard his sharp intake of breath. It felt like forever passed before the sound of his heavy footsteps broke through the drumming of blood in her head.

She didn't drop her hands until she heard the French windows close. When she opened her eyes she found Barney and Rufus sitting beside her, both gazing at her with mournful expressions.

Emiliano, slumped on his late father's sofa, raised bleary eyes when his brother got unsteadily to his feet. They'd been holed up in their father's study for six hours, drinking to his memory.

'We need food,' Damián slurred.

Emiliano hiccupped. 'Eating's cheating.'

'What?'

'That's what the Brits say.'

'Oh.' Damián flopped back down, took another swig out of the bottle of Scotch then passed it over.

It suddenly occurred to him that he hadn't

seen anything of Damián's lady friend since the party five days ago. 'Where's your Brit gone?'

'Gone.'

'Gone where?'

'Home.'

'Which home?'

'Give me the bottle.'

He pressed the bottle against his chest. 'Not until you tell me which home. One of yours or hers?'

'Hers. Now give me the bottle.'

He passed it over. 'Why her home?'

'She doesn't live with me.'

'How long have you two been together?'

'We're not together.'

'You looked like you were together.' He snatched the bottle out of Damián's hand.

'I paid her.'

'What?' Emiliano missed his mouth and spilled amber liquid over his chin. 'I thought she was an actress?'

'She is an actress. I paid her to pretend to be in love with me.'

'Why?'

'I needed help finding Father's will. I thought you'd hidden it somewhere.'

On that score, Emiliano had been right. He didn't blame Damián for thinking that. 'I guessed Celeste had taken it.'

'Did you?'

'You were hardly likely to have hidden it, were you?'

Damián shrugged. 'I can't believe she burned it.'

'I can.' Now Emiliano shrugged. 'You're single-minded when you want something. She knew you'd find it if she didn't destroy it.'

Five days had passed since they'd discovered the extent of their mother's wickedness. She'd disappeared after they'd confronted her with the evidence on the night of the party, escaping on her friend's helicopter. But there would be a day of reckoning for her. On this, as on so many other things now, the Delgado brothers were united. Together, they'd handed all their evidence to the Monte Cleure police and an arrest warrant had been duly issued. They didn't expect her to be charged, not just because the evidence was all circumstantial, but because Celeste knew too many secrets about Monte Cleure's ruling class and wouldn't hesitate to remind those in power of it. The woman who'd taught her sons to always think like chess players, to anticipate and mitigate all eventualities, was the greatest strategist of all.

But should she step foot on Monte Cleure soil again, which she would eventually have to do as the villa was the only home in her name, all the other assets being held in their father's name, she would have the indignity of being arrested. Emiliano fervently hoped the world's press were there to witness it and report that the great Celeste Delgado was suspected of murdering her own husband.

'Do you know what else I can't believe?' Damián slurred.

'What?'

'That I'm sitting here and getting drunk with my brother.'

'Strange, huh?' Emiliano passed the bottle back. 'We should do this more often.' In the drunken fog of his mind, a part of him ached at all the wasted years spent loathing his brother. He didn't want to rewrite history by dissecting the past. Things had been said that could never be unsaid. The guilt in his guts was something he would have to learn to live with but, for the first time, he wanted the brotherly relationship he'd always denied them.

Despite all the alcohol he'd drunk, he felt cold. Snatching the bottle, he took another long swig and tried not to let his mind slip back to the night his body had been chilled to the bone and the woman who'd warmed him.

Other than to pass his boys between them, he'd seen nothing of Becky since she'd ordered him out of her staff lodge. With so many things of a business and personal nature to sort out with his brother, not thinking of her had been easy by day. Only drinking stopped him thinking of her by night too. He didn't want the time or space to think—not about Becky, not about Celeste, not about his adoptive father and all the things he would never get to say to him for good or ill.

But Becky refused to stay hidden. For the little he'd seen of her, she managed to be everywhere. He knew it was his mind playing tricks on him but he would see a figure in the distance and his heart would lunge.

And, just as Celeste would soon face her day of reckoning, for the sake of his liver and the hundreds of staff he employed, he must soon sober up and face the new reality of his life. His mother was a killer and there was the real possibility he'd got one of his employees pregnant.

CHAPTER FIVE

THE TOOT OF the car horn made Becky's stomach clench tightly. Calling the dogs, she pulled her handbag over her shoulder and opened the front door. The dogs went tearing to the car, where Emiliano's driver was putting the suitcase she'd left out front in the boot.

She managed a tight smile when she got into the back and found Emiliano there. She'd hoped he would travel up front.

His smile was equally taut. 'You have everything?'

She nodded and looked away, but not before she'd taken a proper look at his face and found herself shocked at how dishevelled and crumpled his appearance was. She'd hardly seen anything of him since the party six days ago, opening her front door at designated times to either let the dogs out to him or receive them back, rather as she suspected warring parents did for small children. She'd hoped their lack of contact would make being with him again easier to endure but the painful drum of her heart proved that assumption a fallacy. He looked as if he hadn't slept at all since the party. She doubted he'd shaved.

Mercifully, the dogs chose to plonk themselves between the two humans so keeping a good distance from him was made easier.

'There's been a change of plan,' he informed her once the car had set off, his gaze fixed ahead. 'We're going straight to Buenos Aires.'

'Erm... The rest of my stuff's in England.'

'You can collect it when you go back.'

'When will that be?'

'When you've worked your notice. I'll buy whatever you need until then.'

'Have you looked for a replacement for me?'

'I've been busy,' he said shortly.

She stifled a frustrated sigh. 'My notice is up in less than three weeks.'

'I know how a calendar works.'

'I was just...'

'Reminding me.' Clear brown eyes suddenly locked onto hers. 'Reminding me that you're counting down the days until you leave me.'

Taken aback at the way he made it sound as

if she were ending a relationship rather than leaving a job that had only been temporary, and stung at his tone, Becky rested her hand on Barney's head for comfort and looked out of the tinted window in silence until they arrived at the airport.

It was less easy to ignore him on the eighteen-hour flight. The flying time would have been shorter but they made a couple of stops so the dogs could stretch their legs. How Emiliano was able to arrange such things was beyond her, and something she'd stopped being in awe of within days of working for him. Being the possessor of a great fortune, she'd quickly learned, meant the world bent itself to your will rather than the other way round.

It was dark when they landed in Argentina. An hour after leaving the airport and circumnavigating much of the main city itself, the twinkling lights of Luján, a province of Buenos Aires, greeted them from a distance. They reached Emiliano's home before the twinkling lights revealed any of their secrets.

The entire seven hundred hectares of land that made up his estate was fenced off from intruders. Security guards on patrol acknowledged their arrival. Soon they pulled up outside an illuminated sprawling ranch-style mansion. Of the many mansions Emiliano owned, this was the one he considered home.

The stillness of the night was incredible. With the vast black skies covering them and the scent of eucalyptus filling the air, Becky was struck by a sense of wonder that such peace and such space still existed in the world. If she closed her eyes, all she'd hear was nocturnal wildlife, but there was no time for such indulgence as a woman in her mid-thirties stepped out of the front door. Emiliano introduced her as his housekeeper before having a brief conversation in his native language while his driver removed their luggage from the car.

'I'm going to walk the boys to the stables,' Emiliano then informed Becky in a much stiffer tone than he'd addressed his housekeeper. 'Paula's prepared a meal for you. She'll show you to your quarters.' Then he tapped his thigh and strode off, the dogs bounding after him.

Becky exchanged an awkward smile with the housekeeper before following her inside.

Internally, the ranch was even bigger than

she'd expected. Treading over terracotta flooring past a vast split-level living space, she was surprised when Paula went up a flight of stairs, beckoning her to follow. Who had their dining room on a different floor to their kitchen?

That question was answered shortly, when Paula opened a door to reveal a large, beautifully appointed bedroom. 'Your cases been brought up for you,' she said in English. Pointing to a door, she added, 'You living area. Other door bathroom. You like dinner here or downstairs?'

'I think there might have been a mistake. I should be in the staff quarters.' She'd never been housed under the same roof as Emiliano before and knew he had plenty of staff accommodation here.

Paula smiled. 'No mistake.'

'Does Emiliano know?'

'They his orders.'

Exhaustion meant Becky didn't wake until mid-morning. The first thing she did was check her phone to make sure she had no missed calls from Emiliano. He'd messaged her before she'd gone to bed, telling her he'd keep the boys with him that day.

He hadn't tried to contact her while she slept.

Rolling onto her back, she closed her eyes. She'd dreamed of their baby. Only fragments of it remained and, as hard as she tried, she couldn't bring the rest of the dream back.

A rush of protectiveness crashed through her and she placed her hand on her belly, thinking again of the tense conversation she and Emiliano had had the morning after, and with it came the realisation that neither of them had mentioned the pill that could be taken to prevent conception if an accident happened.

Why had that been?

Her emotions had been so erratic back then that she couldn't say if she would have taken it, knew only that if she were to be offered a safe and effective pill now she would refuse it. For all that her hard-worked-for future could be ripped apart, there could be a life growing inside her, a precious, precious life. A baby to share her lonely life and shower all her love on...

Knowing it was dangerous to think like this when there was no way of knowing if she'd conceived, she threw the covers off and headed to the bathroom.

After showering and dressing in her uniform of jeans and shirt, adding an oversized cardigan to the mix as Argentina was currently much cooler than the baking temperatures of Monte Cleure, she headed downstairs in the hope of finding food.

This was the first time since working for Emiliano that she hadn't been given her own cooking facility. It felt strange to be reliant on someone else to be fed.

The ranch was so vast and she'd seen so little of it that, for a moment, she found herself disorientated and unsure in which direction to head. Paula came to her rescue, appearing suddenly to whisk her off to the kitchen.

'You like medialuna?' she asked as she poured Becky a coffee.

'What's that?'

'Breakfast pastries.'

'I love pastries, so yes please.'

Twenty minutes later, Becky was to conclude that she liked pastries a little too much and made a mental note to get the recipe before she returned to England. A cross between a croissant and brioche, the medialunas had a subtle hint of lemon and vanilla to them and she devoured three of them on the bounce and could easily have devoured three more.

She wished she were one of those women who lost their appetite when stressed or unhappy. Becky's appetite only increased, as was evidenced by the roundness of her hips. The past seven years had seen her go from a top-heavy skinny thing to someone with curves to match her breasts.

'What time you like eat lunch?' Paula asked when Becky had finished all the flaky crumbs on her plate.

'That's very kind but I don't want to put you out any more than you've already been. If you show me where everything is, I'll make myself something.'

'You guest. Guest no feed self.'

'I'm not a guest. I'm the dog-sitter.'

'Emiliano say you guest and dog-sitter.'

It was the first time his name had been mentioned between them and Becky's heart skipped a beat to hear it. 'That doesn't sound right,' she said doubtfully. 'Are you sure he meant it like that?'

'Am sure.'

'Very strange… I don't suppose you know where he is, do you?' She asked this as casually as she could.

'He gone see tenants.'

Becky remembered him telling her that he owned adjoining farmland to his estate that he rented out. But that had been in the time before things had become so awkward and tense between them. He seemed to be avoiding her as much as she avoided him, which only made his decision to house her under his roof the stranger. 'Am I okay to explore the estate?'

'Sure. What time lunch?'

'Actually… I don't suppose you have any of those medialunas left I could take with me, have you? Saves you having to bother with lunch for me and, if I'm being honest, I could bury my face in a plate of them and inhale the lot.'

Paula beamed with pride. 'I put in bag for you.'

Becky's long walk ended up being much shorter than anticipated when she found the stables, home to over a hundred and fifty of Emiliano's horses. There, she found many familiar faces from England, who'd recently flown in with the polo horses on specially adapted jets, and ended up sharing her precious medialunas with a couple of the grooms.

'Why aren't you in Greta's old rooms?' Louise asked. 'She used to share with us here.'

She shrugged. 'No idea. Are they still free?'

'We assumed you'd be taking them. You should speak to Emiliano about it. It'd be great to have you with us.'

The stable staff, as friendly and down-to-earth as they were, were such a tight-knit group that Becky flushed with pleasure at the inclusion. In fairness to them, they'd included her from the start but, awkward around new people, she'd initially found it hard to reciprocate. That she'd never had that initial awkwardness with Emiliano had been wholly down to their immediate bonding over his dogs. Besides, his good-humoured nature meant he could befriend the grumpiest hermit. She missed that Emiliano.

And she missed having friends. They used to come so easily to her, but then her happy world had been torn apart and she'd sought solace in her academic work, hardly noticing how insular she'd become. Until she'd started working for Emiliano, she hadn't made a single real friend since her school days. It saddened her to realise she hadn't even noticed.

Her lightening mood lifted some more when she spotted Bertie being walked out of his stable. A former polo horse who'd lost his speed after an injury, Bertie had been kept by Emiliano because Don Giovanni, the most intuitive of his polo horses, pined when separated from him.

Louise must have noticed her joy for she said, 'He needs riding if you fancy it?'

Becky had never ridden a horse prior to working for Emiliano. She'd been wary, frightened of entrusting her safety to such huge creatures, but the grooms had been so kind and supportive that she'd felt compelled to try. Bertie had been the first. He had such a gentle nature and was so intuitive that by the end of her first ride all her fears had disappeared and she'd come to love being on horseback and being at the stables. She'd ridden many of Emiliano's other horses since but Bertie remained her firm favourite.

In no time at all she was astride the stallion in borrowed riding boots and hat. Setting off at a pace as gentle as Bertie himself and with the sun warming her face, the angst that had turned her belly into a mass of knots loosened.

Deciding to explore, she soon found the equestrian circuit, where the dressage and eventers practised and which was used in competitions. A short trot from that were the famous polo fields, six in total, along with practice and schooling areas. Polo fields always looked massive with the players and horses hurtling around them but unoccupied, bar a groundsman on a ride-on mower, they seemed magnified. Vibrant green grass stretched almost as far as her eye could see. After exchanging hand greetings with the groundsman, she figured it was time to turn back.

The stables were as busy as they'd been when she'd set off but a tall figure amongst all the activity immediately caught her attention and her lighter mood plummeted.

Emiliano was back.

The closer she rode, the greater the beat of her heart. The closer she rode, the clearer his features. The clearer his features, the clearer the anger etched on them. She had the distinct impression that anger was directed at her.

Keeping a good distance so she could avoid him until she could be reasonably certain he wouldn't rip her head off, she rode straight to Louise and dismounted before finding the groom who'd loaned her the riding boots.

She was lacing her own boots when a shadow fell over her.

'Enjoyed your ride, did you?'

Taking a deep breath, she lifted her face to his. Somehow she managed to speak over the clatter of her heart. 'Is something wrong?'

Emiliano's fury was so visible she flinched. 'Do you have any idea how dangerous it is to ride a horse in your condition?'

She blinked. 'I beg your pardon?'

'You might have my child growing in you and you think it a good idea to ride a horse? Do you have no sense of self-preservation? Or are you thinking that if you have an accident, nature might take its course and the problem will be over?'

It took a few beats before she understood what he was implying and when comprehension sank in her own temper quickly punched through her.

Keeping her voice as low as she could manage, she snapped, 'We don't know if I'm pregnant or not and even if I am, horse riding is perfectly safe, especially on a gentle horse like Bertie, and how *dare* you imply that I would do *anything* to harm a life?'

Emiliano gazed at the beautiful angry face before him, heart throbbing, head pounding, and tried to get a grip on himself. Staff swarmed around them, a few curious eyes watching.

When Louise had blithely told him Becky had gone for a ride he'd had to stop himself from firing her on the spot. All he'd been able to see was Becky on the ground, helpless. If she hadn't appeared at that moment he would have set off in search of her.

'What if he'd bucked you off?'

'Bertie's softer than a marshmallow.'

But that only brought to mind the softness and taste of her kisses, something he'd fought hard to forget. 'What if he'd been bitten by something? Or trodden on something that lamed him?'

'What if I'd slipped going down the stairs and broken my neck?' she retorted. 'Do you want to ban me from using them on a "what-if?"'

'Don't be flippant. If you're pregnant then it is my job to protect you and our child and that means not allowing you to take any risks with your health.'

'Not *allowing* me?' Her face contorted into a host of incredulous expressions before she got to her feet and hissed, 'Don't you dare lay down the law to me. I'm not a child and I won't tolerate being treated as one. And, while we're on the subject, I understand Greta's old rooms are still available. I want to move into them.'

'Out of the question.'

'Why?'

Because there were no individual staff lodges or cottages here apart from his housekeeper's. Everyone else was housed in the huge staff complex. Because his staff played as hard as they worked. If Becky was carrying his child she needed to rest.

'Because I say so. In case you've forgotten, you are still in my employ until your notice period has been worked and what I say goes.'

Mutiny flared over the beautiful face, plump lips pulling in and out before she deftly side-stepped him and stalked off in the direction of the ranch.

The boys looked from Emiliano to Becky's retreating figure and decided to follow her.

Biting back an oath, Emiliano sucked a huge lungful of air in. When he turned at least a dozen figures suddenly jumped to attention and restarted what they'd been doing before he'd given them cause for diversion.

Damn her, he thought savagely. Damn her for her flagrant lack of self-preservation and damn her for her obstinacy, and damn her for failing to show due deference in front of the other staff. That he'd never expected or wanted deference from staff before mattered not a jot.

'Saddle Nikita for me,' he ordered a passing groom, who started at his tone before hurrying off to comply.

Time for him to go on a long ride of his own.

CHAPTER SIX

BECKY SPENT MUCH of the next week with the boys. She saw little of Emiliano. Their interactions were infrequent and always to the point and always about the dogs. When he'd curtly told her a couple of days ago that he was taking a short trip back to Monte Cleure, she'd breathed an inward sigh of relief.

She tried her hardest not to dwell on their short hate-filled exchange at the stables. But she carried the remnants of it inside her, alternating between hating him for his arrogant, high-handed manner and missing the man he'd been before they'd stupidly slept together. She wished that old Emiliano was still here. The prospect of being pregnant with the old Emiliano's child wasn't as worrying as it was with this closed-off stranger.

And yet, when she'd gone down for breakfast the day before, there had been a hollowness in her chest at his absence. That hollowness hadn't left her. He was due back that evening and every sound had her heart contracting that it could be him.

Feeling as if she would go mad if she rattled around the ranch with only her own thoughts for much longer, she was pleased to get out that evening for a staff party.

It was in full swing when she arrived with the dogs at her side. All the stable staff and other workers were out in force, apart from those doing the night shift—Emiliano did not take any chances when it came to his horses, and the grooms rotated the night shifts—taking full advantage of the chance to let their hair down after a long English polo season and the stressful journey with the horses back to Argentina. Music pumped, beer and wine flowed freely and some of the meat being cremated on the barbecue was actually edible.

Reluctantly, Becky stuck to lemonade. Alcohol was not something she could risk but she still hoped to enjoy herself. Thoughts of Emiliano made that impossible. She couldn't stop her gaze flitting around in dread—or was it hope?—that he'd retuned to the ranch and decided to join the party. Would he stride into the garden armed with kegs of beer and boxes of fine wine, that lopsided grin on his face, lifting the mood even higher with his mere presence as she'd seen him do before?

What was he doing now? Had he gone partying elsewhere? Gone on a date with one of the long-legged beauties who swarmed around him? The thought made her chest tighten painfully, just as it had during all his other absences that week. Strangely, in all the time she'd worked for him, she'd never seen him with a woman on his arm or witnessed a woman scurrying from his home in the early hours.

After a couple of hours of attempting to party, her cheeks hurt from faking smiles and fatigue crept in.

It was a ten-minute walk back but she barely noticed the stars twinkling above her in the dark sky, her thoughts too full of Emiliano and the horrible atmosphere that had developed and been sustained between them. She knew she was as much to blame for it as him. Neither of them had handled their night together and the possible consequences well.

As she approached the ranch she noticed the front porch light was on, a dark figure in shadows. It wasn't until the dogs gave happy barks and bounded forwards, triggering the security lights, that she saw the figure was Emiliano, sitting on a swing chair, a bottle of beer in his hand.

But her heart had already known it was him. One glance at the shadowy figure had been enough for it to thump. For a moment, she was caught unawares enough to soak in his presence, every cavity in her body filling with a mixture of pleasure and pain.

Wearing black jeans and a T-shirt, he looked like the old Emiliano. The crumpled appearance he'd adopted since his mother's party had been smartened up, the dishevelment of his hair now by design rather than neglect. He'd even shaved.

For the first time in a week their eyes locked together. Becky's breath caught in her throat at his searing scrutiny.

He petted his boys then took a long drink from the bottle. 'How was the party?'

She had to untie her tongue to speak. 'Okay. Everyone looked like they were having fun.'

'But not you?'

'No.' She sank onto the wooden step to take

the weight off her weary legs and rested her back against a pillar.

'Why not?'

'Because I'm a day late.'

She heard him suck an intake of breath. 'Is that normal for you?'

'No.' Panic and excitement swelled sharply in equal measure as they did every time she allowed herself to read the signs that were all there. Tender breasts. Fatigue. The ripple of nausea she'd experienced that morning when she'd passed Paula's husband outside and caught a whiff of his cigarette smoke. Excitement that she could have a child growing inside her. Panic at what this meant.

Scared she was going to cry, she scrambled back to her feet. 'Let's give it another couple of days. If I haven't come on by then, I'll take a test.'

She would have gone inside if Emiliano hadn't leaned forward and gently taken hold of her wrist. 'Sit with me.'

Opening her mouth to tell him she needed sleep, she stared into his eyes and found herself temporarily mute.

For the first time since they'd conceived—

and in her heart she was now certain they *had* conceived—there was no antipathy in his stare, just a steadfastness that lightened the weight on her shoulders.

Gingerly, she sat beside him but there was no hope of keeping a distance for Emiliano put his beer bottle down and hooked an arm around her waist to draw her to him.

Much as she wanted to resist, she leaned into him and rested her cheek on his chest.

'Don't be afraid, *bomboncita*,' he murmured into the top of her head. 'We will get through this together.'

Nothing more was said for the longest time and for that she was grateful. Closing her eyes, she was able to take comfort from the strength of his heartbeat against her ear and his hands stroking her back and hair so tenderly. There was something so very solid and real about him, an energy always zipping beneath his skin even in moments of stillness.

He dragged a thumb over her cheek and then rested it under her chin to tilt her face to his. Then, slowly, his face lowered and his lips caught her in a kiss so tender the little of her not already melting to be held in his arms turned to fondue.

Feeling as if she'd slipped into a dream, Becky's mouth moved in time with his, a deepening caress that sang to her senses as she inhaled the scent of his breath and the muskiness of his skin. Her fingers tiptoed up his chest, then flattened against his neck. The pulse at the base thumped against the palm of her hand.

But, even as every crevice in her body thrilled, a part of her brain refused to switch off and it was with huge reluctance that she broke the kiss and gently pulled away from him.

'Not a good idea,' she said shakily as her body howled in protest.

Emiliano gave a look of such sensuality her pelvis pulsed. 'Why?'

Fearing he would reach for her again, she shifted to the other side of the swing chair and patted the space beside her for the dogs to jump up and act as a barrier between them. They failed to oblige. 'Aren't we in a big enough mess?'

Eyes not leaving her face, he picked up his beer and took a long drink. 'That depends on how you look at it. To me, the likelihood that you're pregnant makes things simple. I want you. You want me. Why fight it any more when we're going to be bound together?'

How she wished her heart didn't throb at his admission. And how she wished she could deny that she wanted him too. 'Because it was a one-night stand.'

'A one-night stand that has probably made a baby.'

She raised a helpless shoulder. 'We've hardly been on speaking terms since and the times we do speak we're barely civil to each other.'

Emiliano raised a heavy shoulder in acknowledgement. The past few weeks had been the longest and strangest of his life. The mess with his family would have been enough to screw with his head but the thing with Becky had swirled like a thick mist around him, tying him in a knot of self-recrimination that vied with kernels of excitement that he might be a father. But more potent than all of that was the hunger.

His desire had not kept its distance from her. It breathed in him, in his blood, in his pores, a weight so heavy it threatened to suffocate him.

'It's been a difficult few weeks for me,' he acknowledged. 'I have not behaved as I should. I want to put things right.'

Now that things with Damián were settled, he'd had time to think—something he'd had precious little time for in recent weeks, not in a clear sense. He'd found a clarity that had been missing.

She pressed a hand to her belly. 'Allowing things to become physical will not put things right. It will only muddy the waters more.'

'You mean making love again?' His loins, already tight from their kiss, throbbed at the memory.

'We hardly made love, did we?'

'What would you call it?'

'I don't know.' Her laugh was shaky. 'Whatever it was doesn't matter. If you hadn't been in such a state you would never have come to me and it never would have happened.' She twisted slightly to face him and hesitated before saying, 'What happened to you that night?'

His eyes narrowed. 'You don't know?'

She shook her head.

Sharpness pierced his chest. He'd wondered. Becky was not a woman to gossip. She didn't use social media and only rarely had he seen her use her phone for anything other than making calls. 'You must be the only person in the world who doesn't know,' he said wryly. 'I discovered Celeste killed my father.'

Her eyes widened. 'I thought he passed away in his sleep?'

'Clever, isn't she?' He downed the rest of his beer. So clever and cunning was the woman who'd given birth to him that he was surprised he'd felt any shock when he learnt what she'd done. If the afterlife existed, he doubted his father was up there scratching his head in puzzlement.

And people wondered why he preferred animals to humans!

Coldness had enveloped Becky's brain. She gazed at Emiliano, trying to read his face, desperately hoping he was jesting with her. But what kind of sick joke would that be? 'You really mean it? She killed him?'

He exhaled through his nose and inclined his head, then reached under the swing chair for another bottle and used the attachment on his pocket knife to open it.

She shook her head as nausea swirled violently inside her and her heart wrenched. She'd known something bad had happened that night but never in her wildest imaginings had she suspected anything like this. Who could imagine that?

'I'm so sorry.' What an inadequate platitude.

'So am I. Sorrier that she will never pay the price for it.'

'Why not?'

'All the evidence is circumstantial,' he answered with a shrug. 'Damián hacked the villa's old surveillance feed. He showed me the footage at the party. It shows Celeste carrying a drink from her quarters to my father—this is the woman who has never poured herself a glass of water in her life—and thirty minutes later he was dead. That same night, before his body was cold, she stole his will and a document giving my brother control of the family business. Those documents have been missing since. Presumably, she burned them. The police have seen the footage. They've issued an arrest warrant but unless she confesses there's not enough to charge her, let alone convict her.'

'But that sounds like strong circumstantial evidence.'

'Not strong enough.' He took a swig of his beer. 'My father was cremated. He'd been ill for a long time so his death wasn't unexpected. There was no reason for them to take blood for toxicology. I think even if there was a smoking gun, as it were, she would still get away with it. She knows too many secrets of Monte Cleure's elite. They have to go through the motions of questioning her but she's too big a threat for them to risk charging her.'

She pulled her knees to her chest, trying hard to take everything in. 'Why did she do it?'

He raised his shoulders and rolled his neck. 'For control. She was running out of time to stop Damián taking over the business so took matters into her own hands. You see, she had great influence over Father but on this he was steadfast—he wanted Damián to have it. Damián's a control freak—any influence she had on the business would have been gone—so she killed our father and destroyed the documents with his legal wishes clearly stated because she knew the business would then fall to me.'

'Why?'

'Father had taken Monte Cleure citizenship.

Under Monte Cleure law, if there's no will then the eldest legal son inherits everything. That's me. Celeste knew I wanted nothing to do with the business and that I would pass it to her to run.'

'Would you have?'

'If the truth hadn't come out, yes. And I would have taken great joy in publicly sacking my brother from the company he'd helped make such a great success.'

Her brow creased in disbelief. 'You would be that cruel?'

'Damián and I have hated each other all our lives.' He paused for a moment before correcting himself. 'I have hated *him* all his life. His loathing of me was always a reaction to my own cruel behaviour.'

'Why did you hate him?'

'Many reasons. Jealousy that he was Father's favourite and shared his blood, and then there was Celeste and the poison she dripped in my ear about him. I think she sensed from the moment he was born that he would take her place as Father's chief confidante and went out of her way to make his life as uncomfortable as she could.'

'And I thought my mother was bad,' she murmured but, before he could ask what she meant, she added, 'Do I take it from your tone that you two have made up?'

He nodded and breathed out slowly. 'We met again yesterday at the villa to finalise the legal documents. I've signed the business over to him.'

'The whole business?'

'I never wanted it. From as far back as I can remember I wanted to be outside with the h ses, not stuck in an air-conditioned office.' H d spent more time in the stables at his English boarding school than in the classroom. Even then, he'd preferred animals to humans. Animals were loyal and uncomplicated. Even now he had special distrust for anyone who disliked animals. 'I did work for the business once, a decade ago. I'd been struggling financially—truth is, I'd been living the playboy lifestyle but had no means to earn money for myself. In those days I played for another rich man's polo team and burned through my sponsorship money so quickly it hardly scorched my wallet. I could barely afford to feed the horses. Celeste convinced me to join the business and convinced my father to hire me. He put me in charge of one of the investment funds. I'd worked there six months before he, with Damián's backing, fired me.'

'Why did they do that?'

'It doesn't matter,' he said dismissively. That was something he would never discuss. To remember how his father and brother had treated him in that period was to fill his head with darkness and his guts with poison. He would never forgive them but the grief in his heart for the relationship he'd never had with his father was something he never wanted to experience with his brother. For the sake of his soul he needed to put the past behind him and move on.

'They set up a trust fund for me. Ten million a month for life to keep the hell away from the business. I look back now and see that was the turning point in my life. I was sick of everything. Sick of being financially dependent on them. Sick of being used as a pawn in Celeste's Machiavellian games… I wanted to earn my own living doing the things I love, so I took my hobby and turned it into an empire.' He looked at her. 'I used their first trust payment to get the ball rolling but haven't touched the rest of it. It all goes into a charitable fund for animal causes close to my heart.' He managed a half-hearted grin. 'And causes my father detested.'

'Did you always hate him?'

'Yes.'

She winced at his bluntness.

'He married Celeste because he needed an heir,' he explained. 'She had impeccable lineage, independent wealth and me: proof of her fertility. He adopted me but had no interest in me. Celeste bought me my first pony when I was four. He wouldn't come to the stable so I could show him off—just dismissed it. The only time he gave me attention was when I did wrong.' He grinned, although his heart wasn't in it. 'So I learned to do wrong.'

'That's really sad.'

He snorted. 'Hardly. I had a privileged upbringing. Homes around the world. A fleet of staff just for me. The best education money could buy. Father didn't beat me. He just ignored me. I was a spoilt brat.'

'Can I ask about your real father?'

'He was a polo player like me. He had the potential to be one of the best players in Argentine history but died in a freak horse accident. I was only a baby. I don't remember him.'

'Now that really *is* sad.'

'Sad for him. He never got to see the fantastic man his son would become.'

Amusement suddenly danced in her eyes. 'The fantastic, *modest* man you became.'

'Modesty is my greatest attribute. Apart from my skills as a horseman and a lover,' he added with a wink, and was rewarded with a bright stain of colour across Becky's cheeks before she darted her gaze from him.

Dios, she was irresistible. But he must resist for a short while longer. Until she took the test and the pregnancy was confirmed. Then both their futures would change. They would be bound together always.

She cleared her throat and resolutely said, 'You must get your horse skills from him.'

'Well, I didn't get them from Celeste,' he said drily. 'She only has to look at a horse for it to bolt.'

Her muffled snigger dived straight into loins

already straining against the confines of his jeans.

Emiliano got to his feet. Time for bed before he threw the beautiful creature beside him over his shoulder, carried her to his bedroom and ravished her.

CHAPTER SEVEN

EMILIANO SAT ON the armchair in Becky's bedroom and tried to distract himself by reading through the races he had horses running in that day. While he had limited first-hand involvement in the racing side of his business, he insisted on being kept fully abreast of all goings-on. When he retired from polo-playing he would take a greater hands-on role with the racing side. And the dressage side. He hoped that wouldn't be any time soon but, with his fortieth birthday only two years away, he knew it wouldn't be long until his body started protesting at all the punishment he put it through. He would not be like those polo team owners who let their teams carry them to glory. The moment he stopped pulling his own weight and leading from the front would be the day he hung up his stirrups.

He looked up when the bathroom door opened.

Becky hovered at the threshold, face ashen, hugging herself tightly. She gave a tiny nod.

He dropped his face into his hands and breathed deeply to counteract the sudden rush of blood pounding in his brain. When he looked up, she was still at the threshold of the bathroom. She looked so much like little girl lost that a sharp stab of guilt plunged through him.

Forcing himself to get a grip, he straightened. This was not unexpected. He'd had plenty of time to prepare for this.

Arms still wrapped around her belly, she padded slowly to the other armchair and sank into it. 'What are we going to do?' she whispered.

'That is easy,' he said decisively. 'We get married.'

Her smile was weak. 'Hilarious.'

'No, *bomboncita*, I am serious. I've thought about it a lot and the best thing we can do is marry.'

He'd thought about his childhood. His parents. How he'd hated always being at a distance from them, physically and emotionally. How he wanted no child of his to go through the same. If he was going to be a father then he would be a real father, not some remote authoritarian figure.

And he'd thought about marriage to Becky, about sharing a bed with her every night. Before, when he'd assumed he would spend his life as the eternal bachelor, the mere thought of settling with one woman had made his skin go cold. Circumstance was forcing his hand in this but he did not deny the thought of sharing a bed with this sexy woman who turned him on with nothing more than a look made him feel anything but cold. In many respects, confirmation of the pregnancy was a relief. Becky would be his and in his bed. Why suppress the desire that bound them so tightly when fate had stepped in to bring them together permanently?

He hooked an ankle over his knee while he waited for her to show her relief. Because what was the alternative for her? For their baby?

She slumped back with a long sigh. Her green eyes held his for the longest time. 'I know you mean well but I'm not marrying you.'

He suppressed a smile at the game she'd just started. He knew his wealth made him a prize catch for any woman. But there was always a game to be played. Becky wouldn't want to look too eager to accept his proposal. 'Why not?'

'Because the idea is ludicrous. We hardly know each other.'

'We've known each other for months. We get along great...most of the time.'

She gave a faint smile. 'We don't know each other well at all and we certainly don't love each other.'

'So what? My parents didn't love each other—'

'And look how well that turned out.'

He winced at her well struck barb. 'But they were married for over thirty-five years before Celeste's megalomania got out of control. Some of those years were even happy.'

She arched a brow. '*Some* of them?'

'They were a great team. They both knew the score when they married for what each wanted. It worked very well. There's no reason a marriage between you and me shouldn't work well too.'

'There's lots of reasons.' She started counting off on her fingers. 'One, you're a self-admitted playboy. Two, my parents only married because Mum got pregnant with me—their marriage was never happy. Three, my life is in England and yours is wherever the polo season happens to be.'

Putting his own hands out, he counted off on his own fingers his rebuttals. 'One, if we marry I would do my best to be faithful...'

Her eyes flashed as she interrupted. 'Your best?'

'I will not make a promise I don't know I can keep but I can promise to try.' The way things were going, to feel an attraction for anyone else would be a relief. Since he'd met Becky there hadn't been so much as a kindling of desire for another woman. He didn't know if the two issues were related but, considering how even now, when both their entire futures were being decided, his body thrummed with awareness for her and he couldn't stop his greedy eyes taking in every detail of her beautiful face and fabulous body, he supposed it wasn't an unreasonable theory. 'Two, your parents' marriage is no indication of your own...'

'You used your parents as an example,' she interrupted again with an arch of her brow.

'I'm using the positive side of their marriage as an example,' he corrected.

'There weren't many positives in my parents' marriage, especially the ending of it.'

He fixed her with an exasperated stare at her continued negativity before continuing. 'Three, you would still spend the summer months in England.'

Her eyes narrowed in thought but stayed locked on his. 'Right, so you want me to marry you when you can't guarantee you'll be faithful, when you use our respective parents' disastrous marriages as a template and when I'd, presumably, have to give up my career to follow you around the world?'

'I use my parents' *longevity* as a template. They agreed the score from the beginning and stuck to it. We will do the same. I know the mistakes they made and have no wish to repeat them, and I'm sure you feel the same.'

'The biggest mistake my parents made was getting married in the first place,' she disputed flatly.

'Don't be so negative,' he chided. 'We will forge our own path for marriage.'

'A path that means I'd have to give up my career?' she pressed.

'Children need both parents. Mine were hardly ever in the same country as each other, let alone with me. I want to be involved in my child's life.'

'So you do want me to throw away my career?'

He smiled indulgently. 'When you marry me, *bomboncita*, you will never need to work again.' Under the weight of her darkening stare, he added, 'If you're bored when the baby's older, you can work for my charity—we host many events so your hospitality skills will not be wasted.'

Her green eyes stayed on his face, features tightening as the seconds ticked by. 'You still haven't read my résumé, have you?'

'I prefer to make my own judgements about people.' He'd employed Greta on the basis of her impeccable references and experience with dogs and look what a mess she'd made of things, neglecting the boys to flirt with Juan and any other members of his staff she took a fancy to. He had no issue with his staff bedding each other but only so long as it didn't detract from the job they were paid to do.

He ignored the sly voice in his head that pointed out he'd deliberately housed Becky under his roof here to keep her away from the lusty environment of the stables. That had been out of consideration for her, he told himself staunchly. Nothing to do with being unable to bear the thought of another man even looking at her inappropriately.

She shook her head slowly, grimly. 'This is what I meant about us not knowing each other, although really what I should have said is that you don't know *me*. I don't work in hospitality. I'm a microbiologist.'

Becky felt no satisfaction in seeing the smug smile freeze on Emiliano's face. She wished it didn't hurt that he still hadn't enough curiosity about her to read her résumé, not even after their conversation when she'd written her official resignation. To him, she was just one of many women, interchangeable, forgettable. The only difference between her and the rest of them was that she'd been stupid enough to get pregnant, and she had to push back the heated memories of how much pleasure she'd taken in that stupidity and keep her attention focused on their conversation before she was steamrollered into something she'd regret.

And yet, for the very real catastrophe this pregnancy represented, she could not bring herself to regret it; not the life growing inside her nor the moment of madness that had lit the fuse into its being. The joy that had filled her to see the stick showing positive had been so pure it had almost neutralised the fear. She wanted her baby and already she knew she would do whatever it took to protect and nourish and love it. But that did not mean marrying her baby's father, even if she did find herself weak with longing for him in unguarded moments. If anything, that was another reason not to marry him. With Emiliano, there was just too much danger of losing herself.

'No.' His eyes blinked back into focus. 'That is not possible.'

She shrugged lightly. 'I'm sorry you think that.'

'You were working in a hospitality tent when we met.'

'I was, yes, because I'd finished my doctorate and needed a break from years of brain work.'

He stared at her with the look of a man who'd been earnestly told the earth was flat. 'How the hell can you have a doctorate at your age?'

'By working my backside off. I went straight from my degree into it—I didn't need to do my Master's as I was blessed to get a place on a PhD research scheme. I completed it four months ago. When I go back to England I'll be joining a laboratory in Oxford, working to combat antimicrobial resistance.'

'Anti what?' he asked faintly.

'Antimicrobial resistance,' she repeated patiently. 'In layman's terms, it's what happens when antibiotics and other medicines used to kill infections stop working.'

Time ticked slowly as the handsome face tightened, the clear brown eyes darkening, a pulse throbbing in his temple.

'All this time,' he said in a low voice, 'you've been lying to me.'

'You only had to read my résumé to know all this. Or, you know, ask.'

Emiliano's head had filled with white noise. He'd known Becky wasn't lacking brain cells. That in itself was obvious. But not in a hundred years would he have guessed she was a scientist. To have gained a doctorate at her age suggested an incredibly high IQ and tenacity. Two qualities she shared with his mother and the woman who'd come close to destroying him a decade ago, a thought that cut through the white noise and filled the space with acid. 'You let me believe you worked in hospitality.'

'No, I didn't.' Her tone remained steady. 'I'm proud of what I've achieved and proud of my work. I'll talk about it with anyone who asks. All your stable staff know—ask any of them. It's not my fault your world revolves around yourself and your animals.'

A stab of anger sliced him at this unfounded slur. 'Why work in a hospitality tent at a polo competition?'

She shrugged. 'I told you; I needed to give my brain a break. I was burnt out.'

'But why work there specifically?' At a polo competition, a sport known as the sport of rich men and royalty. Any woman on the search for a wealthy man would be certain to attend… 'How did you hear about the job?'

'This is starting to sound like an interrogation.'

'You're carrying my child. Naturally, I'm curious.' Curious to learn how badly duped he'd been by this woman.

Her eyes held his, the suspicion in his guts mirrored in their reflection. 'My dad used to run a catering company. I called around his old contacts to see who was hiring seasonal workers.'

'Why not go travelling like a normal person suffering burn-out?'

'Most normal people do not have the money to go travelling on a whim.' Her voice had an edge to it. 'I needed money. I'd done bar work to supplement my grant when I was doing my degree but earned nothing while doing my doctorate. I've been pretty much cloistered for the last three years so thought it would be good to mix with people who could hold a conversation about something other than microbes. I didn't figure on them all being drunk. When you offered me the job of dog-sitter I thought all my holidays had come at once.'

He managed a tight smile. 'I'm sure you did.'

'What does that mean?'

'Only that after all those years of hard brain work, being paid to live in a beautiful country estate and walk dogs must have sounded idyllic,' he lied smoothly.

She leaned forward and rested her elbows on her thighs. 'Why does it sound as if you're implying something?'

He raised his shoulders and pulled a nonchalant face. 'Maybe you have a guilty conscience about something.'

Her features were pinched together as she continued studying him. 'Out with it.'

'With what?'

'I can't be doing with insinuations. If you've something to say, say it.'

'I just find it curious that not once, in all the time I've known you, have you mentioned that you're a scientist.'

'You sound like a stuck record—not once did we have a conversation that led to it. There's something else, so go on, spit it out. What else is bugging you?'

'You're an intelligent woman. I'm sure you can work it out.'

'I'm not a mind-reader.'

'And neither am I, which means I have to take on trust that you forgot to tell me you weren't on the pill.'

Her eyes widened. 'You think I forgot deliberately?'

'I didn't say that.'

'Stop with the weasel words,' she hissed. 'We both got carried away in the heat of the moment, so stop blaming me for your own ignorance about my career. Do you know what I find curious? Your inability to deal with being proved wrong. You were angry after we slept together because it hadn't crossed your thick head that I might be a virgin, and here you are again, angry that your image of me as a simple country barmaid has been proved wrong too. Is it just me you don't trust or women in general?'

Her question was so astute that Emiliano found himself in the unedifying position of being wrong-footed. 'I don't trust anyone,' he snapped.

'Then you can doubly forget marriage if that's going to be added to the list of things I'd have to put up with.' Rising to her feet, she glared at him. 'I'm going to take the boys for a walk. Let me know when you're in a less cynical mood—we can discuss things properly then.'

She slammed the door behind her.

* * *

Emiliano rubbed Hildegarde's clever head before handing the reins to a groom. He was about to walk away when the groom asked about the night shift for the forthcoming party. He almost smacked his own forehead at the reminder.

With everything that had been going on in his life he'd completely forgotten about the party he was hosting in a couple of weeks for his polo team and all their respective staff. It had been the most successful English season they'd ever played in and it was only right he reward them for it, but a party was something he could do without right now. He needed to devote his energy to convincing Becky to marry him. And it wasn't just the party. The break he'd given his team came to an end in a few days and practice would resume; new ponies needed to be tested, the new player he'd signed needed to bed into the team and then there were the myriad issues that needed dealing with on the non-playing side of the business and the worry of a sickness that had infected a significant number of his horses in the Middle East.

How could he concentrate on any of this when the woman carrying his child was proving herself an enigma and refused to do the right thing and marry him?

As he thought this he suddenly spotted Becky walking past the stables, his boys obediently at her side. As if she sensed his stare, she turned her face to him and stopped. Across the distance their gazes locked and held.

His chest filled, cramping his lungs, forcing him to drag in a deep breath of air. All the anger that had been simmering in him since she'd stormed out of her bedroom three hours ago, anger that hadn't abated even after a long ride on Hildegard, left him.

He barely registered putting one foot in front of the other. One minute they'd been hundreds of yards from each other. The next, he was standing in front of her.

A strand of hair not tied back in her ponytail caught in the breeze. He locked his hands behind his back to stop his fingers reaching for it.

'That was a long walk,' he murmured.

She just stared at him. Her throat moved

a couple of times before she said quietly, 'I needed thinking time.'

He knew that feeling.

'Hungry?' he asked.

The beginnings of a smile played on her lips. 'Starving.'

'Then let's get lunch.'

They walked in silence until they were out of earshot of the stables. After his long, vigorous ride, the cooling breeze was welcome. It couldn't cool the baser part of him though, he conceded ruefully, not when Becky was within touching distance.

'What did you think about on your long walk?'

Becky took her time before answering because there was no easy answer to give. She'd spent most of the walk fuming over his implication that she'd deliberately got pregnant and fuming over his reaction to finding out about her career. His arrogant assumption that she would be happy to commit herself to marriage with an unfaithful husband—a promise to 'try' was, in her view, an insult and, worse, a stab to a heart already filled with far too much emotion than was healthy for a playboy like Emiliano Delgado. And then she'd remembered all the family stuff he'd been dealing with and her anger had turned to an ache that made her want to cry for him.

How did he do that? How could he anger her to such a pitch that her head could explode with rage then tug at her heartstrings enough for her to weep? And how, stronger than her anger or empathy, was it that just to look at him was enough for her to fill with so much heat it felt as if her bones were melting?

'Everything and nothing,' she finally settled on.

'Evasion, *bomboncita*?'

Hating that her heart skipped a beat to hear that caress from his lips, she studiously kept her gaze fixed ahead and fought to keep her voice steady. 'Not deliberately.'

'Are you still angry with me?'

'No…' She couldn't resist turning her face to look at him for a brief moment. 'Well, a little.'

'That's encouraging.'

She couldn't help the laugh that escaped to hear the old playful tone in his voice.

But then the serious mood returned. 'You know, I have never thought before about how I react to surprises.'

'What do you mean?'

'What you said earlier, about my reaction to your virginity—don't think I didn't notice you confirmed that for me—and to your job. I reacted badly both times. I will try to do better.'

Her heart gave a little thump. 'Is that your way of apologising?'

'I wouldn't go that far but I can admit when I'm wrong.'

'Go on then.'

'Go on, what?'

'Admit you were wrong.'

'My reaction was wrong.'

'And your insinuation that I intentionally got pregnant?'

Emiliano's guts plunged. He reached out for her hand and, holding it firmly, stopped walking. He could only assume it had been wounded pride at her dismissal of his proposal that had made him lash out like he had. He wished he could still believe she'd been playing a game but he was not one to indulge in self-delusion. Becky had been a virgin. She hadn't deliberately set out to trap him.

And she didn't want to marry him.

But that didn't mean he had to accept it. People could change. Minds could be changed. He'd never backed away from a challenge in his life and wasn't about to start now.

'Wrong. For that, I do apologise.'

She stared at their clasped hands before slowly raising her eyes to his. 'I would never do that.'

'Many women would.'

'I'm not many women.'

'No,' he agreed. The breeze had caught that stray lock of hair again. This time he didn't resist, smoothing it off her face with the hand not holding hers. If he hadn't been studying her so closely he would have missed the little quiver his touch evoked. He stepped even closer to her. 'You are not like other women.'

'Not like the other women you normally sleep with, you mean,' she corrected, but with a hitch in her voice that gratified him as much as her quiver had done. It emboldened him, made clear the route he needed to take to extract the change of mind he wanted from her. That it was the most pleasurable route only made it the sweeter.

'That is possible.'

'I'd say it's definite.'

'You have been studying my previous lovers?'

'There's not enough hours in the day to do a comprehensive study.'

'There has been no one since you.' No one since she'd come into his life…

'Is that supposed to be a compliment?'

'Just a fact.' He slipped an arm around her waist and drew her flush against him. 'Just as it is a fact that I have never desired a woman more than I desire you.' He put his mouth to her ear. 'Tell me it's not the same for you.'

'I…' Becky unclasped her hand from his and pressed it against his chest, ready to push him away, but found her fingers grabbing hold of his polo shirt. The heat of his breath against her ear was doing crazy things to her, and when he took advantage of her loss of words to press feather-light kisses over her face, everywhere but her mouth, she was saturated with a desire so strong it was a struggle to even breathe.

Somehow she summoned the strength to let go of his shirt and step out of his reach. 'Please, we agreed…' God, she could hardly get her voice working.

'Agreed what?'

'Not to muddy the waters with…this.'

His eyes gleamed. 'I promised no such thing.'

'Then make that promise.'

'No.'

'Please, Emiliano, I don't want us to be at war, but…'

'I prefer to make love not war.'

She was saved from having to think of a response to words that made her abdomen clench by a huge pick-up truck stopping beside them. It was Emiliano's head groundsman, offering them a lift back to the ranch.

Snatching at this gift of respite, she practically flew into the passenger side. She could have screamed when Emiliano followed her in and she was forced to share the two-seat space with him and the dogs, who obediently sat themselves in the footwell. Space upfront was so tight and Emiliano so big that their bodies were tightly compacted together, thigh pressed against thigh, side against side. She folded her arms tightly across her chest but that did nothing to dull the wanton heat flushing through her.

God help her, she prayed. Help her before she self-combusted.

CHAPTER EIGHT

THE RIDE BACK to the ranch took barely two minutes. For Becky it felt like hours, time suspended in a closed environment where her senses were filled with the heat of Emiliano's body pressed against her own and the earthy scent of his fresh sweat. It was torture.

When they pulled up outside the front door, Emiliano thanked Gabriel before jumping out. Murmuring her own thanks, Becky budged over to get out too but, before she knew what he was planning, Emiliano's strong hands were at her waist and he was lifting her out of the truck as if she weighed nothing at all.

He set her gently to the floor. Legs weakened, she had to fight not to sway into him. Hands lingering at her waist, his eyes gleamed as he leaned in to murmur into her ear, 'I'm going to take a shower before we eat.'

There was no relief when he released his hold

on her waist and bounded into the ranch, not when every part of her ached and throbbed.

Inside, all was quiet. Or was it the steady beat of blood in her head deafening her?

She couldn't stop her gaze from following him up the wide staircase, the longing to follow him with more than her eyes more than she could bear. With a wrench, she turned on her heel and hurried to the kitchen for company that wasn't hunky Argentinian male. But the kitchen was empty of everything but the scent of cooking.

She poured herself a coffee from the prepared jug on the counter but her hands shook so much that when she tried to take a sip of it, it spilled over her shirt. She snatched at a tea towel and dabbed as much of it as she could, thankful that she liked her coffee half-filled with milk. Her skin already felt burned.

Needing to change her wet shirt, she approached the stairs with trepidation. To get to her room she had to pass Emiliano's, a fact she'd studiously tuned out every other time she'd walked past it.

This time it was impossible to tune out, especially when she found the door partially open.

An invitation? The mere thought was enough for her knees to weaken all over again.

Why was she hovering there? And why was her hand reaching forward…?

'You can come in, you know,' a deep voice drawled from the other side of the door.

Immediately she pressed her shaking hand to the place where her heart would have been if it hadn't jumped to her throat.

The door opened fully. Emiliano, still dressed, lopsided smile on his face, eyes dark and knowing, swept an arm behind him in invitation.

'I was on a call with my English vet,' he explained casually, as if finding Becky hovering outside his door was an everyday occurrence.

She had no recollection of crossing the threshold or closing the door behind her.

Since their night together, Becky had kept a firm control of herself, aware of her susceptibility to him, aware that he'd left his mark on her in a deep-rooted way that had nothing to do with the pregnancy. She'd believed the awareness of her desire made it controllable.

She'd been a fool, she now realised hazily. The distance they'd both imposed had been the thing keeping it controlled. Now that Emiliano had breached that distance and turned those laser eyes and the full weight of his desire back on her, the walls she'd erected around herself had come crashing down. For the first time she could admit that she didn't want to build them back up and she didn't want to fight it any more.

Emiliano was right. They were going to be bound together for ever so why fight the inevitable? The longing in her blood made the inevitability clear to her.

And now she was in his room, trembling with nerves and excitement, her senses too overloaded with Emiliano to even give his inner sanctum a cursory glance. All she could see was him. All she could hear was her own heartbeat.

'Join me in the shower?' he said in that same casual tone before he pulled his polo shirt over his head.

Her mouth opened but nothing came out. She had no idea what she would have said even if speech had been possible.

Eyes back on her, he pinched the sides of his jodhpurs and without a modicum of shame pulled them down to his feet, stripping his underwear as he went.

Naked, barely feet away, he stared at her.

And all she could do was stare back, drinking in every part of his masculine perfection. She remembered so well the feel of him naked on her and in her, but to see him in the light took what little breath she had left away.

The lean yet muscular body she'd imagined vividly was so much more. Of everything. Harder. The shoulders broader, the biceps more muscular, the thighs more powerful. A smattering of dark hair whorled in the centre of his chest, narrowing to a thin line down his flat abdomen then thickening to where his erection jutted out as hard and as big as the rest of him.

Brown eyes darkening, he watched her soak him in.

'Your turn,' he rasped with a flare of his nostrils.

Her hands moved with no connection to her brain. Surprisingly steady, they opened the buttons of her shirt one by one before she shrugged the sleeves off. And then she moved to her jeans.

Emiliano's throat had run dry. Never in his

life had he been as mesmerised as he was in that moment. He'd climbed the stairs to his room with Becky's dazed yet hungry eyes following him but no expectation that *she* would follow. He'd learned the hard way with Becky to expect the unexpected.

And now she was in his room, stripping off her clothes. Shyness had brought a blush to her cheeks but her beautiful green eyes, pulsing with unconcealed desire, did not waver. It was the most erotic sight he had ever seen.

He barely suppressed a groan when she stepped out of her jeans. The groan came unbidden when she unhooked her bra and released the breasts whose taste he remembered with crystal-clear clarity but whose image were shadowed.

And then she tugged her knickers down too.

He gritted his teeth and breathed deeply through his nose. *Dios*, a man could die and go to heaven in that curvy softness.

She was like a milkmaid of medieval times. Creamy weighty breasts were topped with perfect raspberry nipples, the hips wide and rounded, belly softly rounded, a cloud of soft dark hair in the arrow between legs much smoother and shapelier than he'd dreamed. *Everything* was more beautiful and perfect than he'd dreamed.

And he'd dreamed about her, waking and in sleep, so many times he'd lost count.

The dream was perfected when she pulled the hairband out and her chestnut waves came tumbling down.

Breathing deeply, he extended a hand.

Eyes not breaking contact with his, she reached out to take it. A spark of electricity pulsed through him at the first touch.

Becky let Emiliano lead her into the huge walk-in shower in his bathroom. The way she felt right then, she would have let him lead her anywhere. Any embarrassment at being naked in the light with a man for the first time had gone when she'd seen the effect it had on him. The heat in his eyes alone could power a station.

She let him position her under the wide shower head, facing him. He stretched an arm to press a button on the wall. An instant later, water at a perfect temperature rained down on them. She shivered at the effect it had on her highly sensitised skin then held her breath as she waited for what he would do next.

He turned slightly to fill his hands with gel from the dispenser on the wall and then, eyes on hers, lathered his magnificent body, cleaning every part he could reach. When he took hold of his manhood to clean that too, Becky experienced such a deep throb of longing that her lungs stopped functioning.

Eyes now hooded, he rasped, 'Turn around.'

Trembling with anticipation, she obeyed.

He gathered her hair and tucked it to one side over her shoulder before she heard him fill his hands with more gel. In slow, rhythmic movements, he washed every inch of her back, from the nape of her neck all the way to the base of her spine. When he gently massaged the gel into her buttocks she shot a hand out against the wall to keep herself upright.

Already lost in a bubble of desire, when he gripped her hips and pressed himself against her, his erection hard against her lower back, and growled seductively into the top of her head, she was helpless to stop the moan of need flying from her lips.

And then he gently turned her to face him.

Breathing heavily, he gazed into her eyes for the longest time before reaching again for the gel. He lathered his hands then placed them on her shoulders. His Adam's apple moved before he slowly lathered her arms, all the way to her fingers, then back up and around to the base of her throat before massaging her breasts.

The sensations his seductive caresses were firing through her were too strong to sustain. Her legs were shaking. But the caresses were relentless and when he'd finished massaging her belly and gently moved lower she would have fallen to the floor if he hadn't hooked an arm around her waist and carefully steered her to the deep tiled ledge running along the left of the vast space and helped her sit. The shower head must have moved by sensor for the spray followed them.

Dropping to his knees before her, Emiliano continued to lather her body. His strong hands massaged the gel into her thighs and calves then lifted each foot in turn and rubbed his thumbs into her soles and toes. All the while, the heavy sting of the shower drenched her skin, adding to the sensation filling her.

When every inch of her had been cleaned, he put a hand on each ankle then brushed all the way back up until he was gripping her hips and his eyes were staring into hers.

His breathing was as erratic as her own, she thought dimly, but it was the last coherent thought in her pleasure-saturated mind for he captured her lips in a kiss of such savage passion that she melted into him with abandon.

Her hand cradled the back of his head, fingers kneading as their tongues entwined in a fierce erotic dance that only fed the burning need inside her. When he hooked an arm around her waist to pull her flush against him and her breasts pressed against his hard torso, the burn in her pelvis turned into a throb that had her moaning for relief from the exquisite pain.

As if sensing her need, Emiliano broke the kiss to brush his lips over her cheeks and then down the side of her neck, sinking lower as his mouth moved over her aching breasts and captured the erect tips whole in turn. Oh, the *sensation*…

His mouth continued its erotic assault of

her flesh. His appreciative groans stoked her responses, an instinctive knowledge that for every ounce of pleasure he was giving her, he received gratification too. By the time he reached the essence of her femininity she was so far gone in the thick haze of desire that when he pressed his mouth to it and inhaled deeply she grasped wildly for his hair to cling to, tilted her head back to rest against the wall and closed her eyes.

With one hand clasping her hip and the other roaming over her belly and breasts, his tongue stroked her with an incessant pressure that had her reaching a peak in moments.

Then, no sooner had the waves of rippling pleasure begun to ebb than Emiliano moved his mouth to kiss his way back up over her belly and breasts to her lips, his tongue plunging back into her mouth at the same moment he plunged deep inside her.

Emiliano groaned loudly and stilled. *Dios…*

How he held himself together he would never know. Their first time together had been an explosion of passion with no time to savour or appreciate. This time, he wanted to savour the intensity of every perfect moment but it was hard when he was buried deep in Becky's tight heat and the weight of her perfect breasts pushed against his chest and the taste of her lingered so deliciously on his tongue. His senses were infused by so many intoxicating sensations that he had to grit his teeth tightly to stop the climax begging for release.

He kissed her, long and hard. And then he began to move.

Every thrust, every brush of her breast, every breathy moan that poured from her into his mouth, every knead of her fingers into his flesh fed the hunger in him. In and out he thrust, harder and harder, being pulled deeper and deeper into the abyss, clinging on by his teeth as Becky's movements became more frantic too and her moans deepened and then, just as he feared he could hold on no more, she pressed tightly against him with a cry that seemed to come from her very soul and shuddered wildly in his arms.

And then he was lost. His climax ripped through him, pleasure flooding him so thoroughly that, for the longest moment, the world around him turned into flickering white.

* * *

Slowly, the second wave of pulsations to have crashed through her settled and Becky drifted back to earth.

Her face was buried in Emiliano's neck and when she turned to breathe she was surprised to find the shower still spraying over their fused bodies.

When he shifted she held her only just regained breath as the aftermath of their first coupling suddenly played in her mind. When he moved the arm wrapped so tightly around her, fear swiftly clutched her heart.

She didn't think she could bear it if the beauty of what they'd just shared was tarnished with anger and recriminations. Not again.

Only when the shower stopped did she realise he'd moved so he could turn it off, but her relief lasted seconds for he pressed his lips to her forehead before pulling out of her and getting to his feet.

Cold at the abrupt loss of his heat and suddenly self-conscious of her nakedness, she pressed her thighs together and twisted away, afraid to look at him.

Becky heard him walk away and squeezed

her eyes shut. She must not cry. Not until she was in the privacy of her own room with the door locked.

She kept them closed even when she heard his footsteps near her again, bracing herself.

A hand slid between her back and the tiled wall and gently pulled her forward, then the softest, warmest, fluffiest towel was wrapped around her. Strong arms held her securely before she was lifted up and carried effortlessly into the bedroom.

There, Emiliano sat her on the sofa and pressed another kiss to her forehead. 'Wait one second,' he murmured in a hoarse voice.

When he returned from the bathroom he'd wrapped a towel around his waist and carried another in his hands. He sat beside her and put the fresh towel against her hair. Working with infinite patience and without a single word being exchanged, he towel-dried it in sections until her chestnut locks no longer dripped everywhere.

Done, he stared at her before placing a finger under her chin and pressing a tender kiss to her mouth.

'I shall get food. Don't go anywhere,' he said in the same hoarse voice.

She nodded, still too choked with emotion to speak.

He disappeared into his dressing room, re-emerging wearing a pair of faded jeans and carrying a maroon towelling robe. He handed it to her with a smile before giving her another kiss and strolling out of the door.

Alone, Becky took a minute to gather herself before slipping into the giant robe. It trailed to her ankles and the sleeves needed rolling three times to stop them dangling past her hands, and yet there was something comforting and intimate in wearing something that was his. Gathering her towels into her arms, she carried them to the bathroom to hang on the towel-warmer, aware with every step of the tenderness between her noodly legs.

She looked in the mirror. The flushed face staring back at her had the dazed look of someone who'd been made love to.

CHAPTER NINE

EMILIANO CARRIED THE tray piled high with food up the stairs, his heart beating more forcefully as he neared his bedroom. He only understood they'd been the beats of dread when he pushed the door open and relief washed through him to find Becky still there and curled up on the sofa. His heart bloomed when she lifted her head and smiled.

'I bring us a feast,' he announced as he placed the tray on the low table by the sofa.

Her eyes lit up. 'Medialunas.'

He grinned and sat beside her. Just in case she was inclined to move away from him, he grabbed her ankles and placed them on his lap, and was gratified when she didn't resist. 'Paula told me you have taken a liking to them.'

He'd also filled the tray with the fruits she liked and, after much head scratching, worked out how to make a fresh pot of coffee, which he'd balanced with the rest of the stuff. He could have called Paula or another member of his household staff to do it for him, but he'd had a strange compulsion to do it himself.

'I could scoff them all day.'

'I could scoff *you* all day,' he replied with a suggestive wink that made her blush.

After the way things had been between them the first time they'd made love, it loosened the knots in his guts to have things back on an even keel with her. Not that things had ever been *even* as such. Not with Becky. Right from the start there had always been that undercurrent of desire between them which they had both ignored with explosive results, leading to anger and recrimination but always, *always*, that desire burning brightly, waiting to be unleashed again.

To make her smile, to see her blush, to have her feet resting on his lap as if that was where they belonged…

Taking care not to hurt her feet, he leaned forward to pile a plate of pastries and fruit for her before sorting his own plate out and pouring the coffee.

As he devoured his first medialuna whilst observing Becky's more delicate approach, he had to concede this was the lightest he'd felt in a long time, certainly since the party that had seen his world fall apart, possibly even since his adoptive father had died.

'So, my little microbiologist,' he said teasingly. 'Tell me, were you a swot at school?'

Her pink tongue darted to the corner of her mouth and a tiny flake of pastry stuck there disappeared. 'I was the biggest swot going.'

'And were you always interested in germs?'

She raised her brows and pulled a bemused face. 'I wasn't a complete oddball.'

'So why specialise in them?'

'I'd actually intended to do a chemistry degree but I went to a university open day to get a feel for the place and got talking to a student doing a degree in microbiology. It just sounded really exciting so I applied and that was that.'

Now he was the one to pull a bemused face. 'Germs sounded exciting?'

'Bacteria, viruses, fungi and protozoa,' she corrected with a grin that made him want to kiss her until she ran out of air. 'And yes, it did sound *hugely* exciting to me—the course, I mean. And the career it could lead to.'

'And what will you be doing in your new

job?' Privately, he hoped it would be something unimportant and inconsequential, a role she could turn her back on to spend her life with him. And their baby, of course, he quickly reminded himself.

She stretched her ankles and wiggled her pretty toes. 'I'll be joining a team working on inhibiting efflux pumps.'

'And they are…?' He did his best to sound interested but internally he was already partying in his head, celebrating that it did indeed sound unimportant and inconsequential.

'Think of them as naturally occurring minuscule pumps that sit on bacterial cells sucking out toxic substances. When you take antibiotics for infections, they're the blighters sucking *out* the antibiotics from inside the cells, essentially booting out the cure before it can get to work. If we can inhibit the efflux pumps then it will reduce the bacteria's ability to boot out the antibiotics and, hopefully, make the antibiotics effective again.'

The internal partying came to an abrupt halt. That did not sound either unimportant or inconsequential. Damn it.

'Think of the implications if we're successful,' she said quietly, her eyes holding his. 'It's not just humans that will benefit but the animal world too. Antibiotics are becoming less effective for all creatures. Horses too.'

And didn't he know it. Emiliano spent a small fortune vaccinating his horses and taking all the other preventative measures available to keep them free from disease but not everything could be prevented. In his world there was much awareness and fear of antibiotic resistance.

How the hell was he going to convince her to put work of such importance to one side and join him on the polo circuit with their child, to marry him, to be a family, without sounding like a selfish oaf?

The answer came to him. It would be done carefully. With stealth.

Taking her empty plate, he placed it on the table and exchanged it for her coffee. 'What's the maternity package at your company like?' he asked casually.

She took a sip of the coffee and wrinkled her nose. 'I don't know. It's in the company handbook but that's in England with the rest of my stuff. I'll read up on it when I go back next week.'

'You don't have to go back so soon.' He seized the open goal with gusto. 'Why not stay until your new job starts?' That would give him a few extra precious weeks to work his magic. For good measure he added, 'You can help me select your replacement.'

'I can't. I've got too much to organise.'

'Such as?'

'For a start, I need to buy furniture for my flat. And cooking utensils, crockery... You name it, I need to buy it.'

'I will get them for you.'

'No.'

'Yes,' he countered firmly. 'And when you say flat, do you mean something small and poky?'

'Compared to the homes you're used to then yes, but for a normal person it's fine.'

'How about for a normal person with child?'

'I'll manage.'

'No, *bomboncita*, you won't but we have plenty of time to sort that. The most pressing thing for now is to get your flat furnished. I will take you shopping tomorrow. You can choose whatever you want and I'll have it couriered to England and installed in the flat for when you return. Problem solved, see? You can stay here longer.'

Becky narrowed her eyes. His generosity didn't surprise her—Emiliano was unfailingly generous—but, even though her heart sang loudly to think of staying another three weeks with him, she had to be practical and not look at things with sex-sated eyes. Emiliano never did anything that wasn't to his own advantage. 'Don't bulldoze me,' she warned.

'It is not bulldozing,' he said with a disappointed tut. 'It is using my wealth to my own advantage to keep you in my bed for as long as I can.'

She almost laughed at this admittance so closely following her private thoughts. 'What do you mean by *in your bed*?'

'You're moving in here with me,' he told her cheerfully. 'And do not argue. If you won't move your stuff over, I'll do it myself.'

She finished her coffee, her brain racing. She got why he wanted her to stay longer but it hadn't occurred to her that he would actually want her to share his private space with him, even if only on a semi-permanent basis. From all the gossip she'd heard from the grooms, who got all their titbits from his various household staff across the globe, Emiliano had an aversion to women spending more than a night with him. It was a standing joke that come the morning, he would offer them breakfast and then a taxi. It was the standing joke that had made her determined never to act on her attraction to him.

'You want me to share your bedroom while I'm here?' she clarified, in case her thoughts had gone a little too wayward.

He held his hand out for her mug. 'What I want is for you to get it into your clever head that you and I are together.'

Her heart jumped so hard that if the mug she placed in his waiting hand had been full it would have spilt all over him.

'Together?' she echoed faintly.

'A couple.' He put the mug on the table then put his hands back on her ankles and pulled her flat. His eyes gleamed as he stared down at her. 'Change your social media settings to "In a Relationship".'

'I'm not on social media.'

He slipped a hand in the gaping front of his robe, still wrapped around her, and cupped a fabulously full breast. 'But you are in a relationship, so get used to it. You are my woman and I am your man and together we will find a solution to raise our child together.'

'Emiliano...' She sighed, torn between wanting to move his hand away so she could think properly and wanting him to carry on his wonderful caress. 'I said I didn't want to marry you.'

'Who said anything about marriage?' he asked with an innocent look that immediately made her think he was lying. 'I just think we owe it to our baby to try. Or do you disagree?'

Before she could answer, he dipped his head and took a nipple in his mouth.

Her sigh this time was one of pleasure, a sigh that turned into a moan when he pulled the robe apart completely to kiss and caress her other breast, hazily aware he was tugging his jeans down at the same time. She sank into the pleasure he was giving and groped for him, clutching at his hair, a deep ache between her legs which he gently parted as he kissed his way back up to her neck and nestled himself between.

His erection pressed at the top of her thigh as his face hovered over hers, brown eyes gleaming with lust. Those sensual lips would have fused against hers if she hadn't finally found the sense to turn her face.

'I don't want to be rushed into anything,' she managed to say breathlessly, even though he'd slid a finger inside her and her pelvis had arched into his hand in automatic response. 'You're like a bulldozer when you want something.'

His thumb pressed against her nub, making her gasp. 'All I'm asking is for you to give us a chance.'

She turned her face back to gaze into his eyes and found her back arching so her breasts could press against his chest. 'Only if you promise to be faithful.'

'I will be faithful for as long as we're together,' he promised solemnly, slowly moving his hand away and pressing his erection to her. 'Now will you agree to move your stuff into my room?'

'Why do I feel like I'm being manipulated?'

He slid deep inside her with a long drawn out groan. 'Because, *bomboncita*, you're a very clever woman.'

'It is *what*?'

'A slow cooker,' Becky explained with a patience she was fast losing.

'How does it work?'

She shook her head, amusement suddenly replacing the exasperation. Every kitchen item she'd looked at in the Trapani Department Store Emiliano had brought her to had been met with questions. It was like going shopping with an overly curious toddler. Except Emiliano was a fully-grown man who'd never cooked a meal in his life. 'It cooks food slowly. It means I can chuck stuff in it before I go to work and then it will be all cooked and delicious when I get home.'

'I'll hire you a chef.'

'I don't need a chef. I need a slow cooker.' And she needed to find a way to at least contribute towards all the stuff he was buying for her.

If she'd realised he was taking her to a department store that only catered for the filthy rich she'd have insisted on going to one that catered for the opposite end of the financial spectrum. It wasn't until she'd sat on a sofa so comfortable she imagined it was used up in heaven and then looked at the price tag and almost had a heart attack that she'd understood just how astronomically expensive it all was here. She'd jumped off it and was on the hunt for a cheaper one—fat chance, she'd quickly learned—when Emiliano had appeared at her side and smugly told her it was hers. When she'd tried to get around his generosity by refusing to look at bedroom furniture, he'd fixed her with a look and said if she didn't choose stuff for herself, he would choose for her. When she'd then begged him to take her somewhere cheaper, he'd fixed her with that same look and said, 'I will not have the mother of my child putting up with second-rate stuff when I can afford the best.'

'But I don't need Egyptian cotton sheets with a thousand threads,' she'd protested.

'You might not, but I do.' He'd then put his mouth to her ear and added, 'Believe me, *bomboncita*, I will be sharing the sheets with you whenever I can.'

She'd had to press her thighs together to counteract the throbbing warmth his seductive words had roused and hoped no one could see the flush of colour staining her cheeks. The plan for him to take her shopping had been delayed by two days as, other than taking the dogs for long walks together, they'd found it impossible to drag themselves out of bed.

They had been the most heavenly days of her life.

They moved on from the slow cooker—Emiliano patted it to let the poor sales assistant tasked with helping them know they wanted it—and, after selecting a coffee machine, Becky found the utensils. She laughed to find a fish slice here cost as much as a slow cooker would have done in a reasonably priced store.

'Why don't you already have these things?' Emiliano asked while Becky dithered over which knife set she wanted.

'I lived in student digs when I was doing my degree but the university I did my doctorate at was close enough to my mum's for me to commute, so I moved into her annexe. My parents built and furnished it for my grandmother. She lived in it until she became too fragile and had to move into a care home.'

'You can show me it when you introduce me to your parents.'

She grimaced. 'We'll see. Anyway, that's me done here. I've enough to get started in the flat. Can we get something to eat now?'

But a kernel of distrust had unfurled in Emiliano at the expression on Becky's face. 'You don't want me to meet them?'

He had yet to spend more than a night with a woman without her hinting about meeting the parents, despite him making it very clear that what they were sharing was sex and only sex. Adriana was the only woman whose parents he'd wanted to meet. Only when they were over had he discovered why she'd resisted this—to stop him learning the truth about her. By then it was too late. The titanic damage had been done.

'My dad's in Europe somewhere having a midlife crisis,' she said, her tone shorter than he was used to.

'And your mother?'

She shrugged. 'We don't speak any more.'

'Why not?'

'For reasons I'm not discussing in the middle of a department store. Can we get some lunch?'

'Only if you let me buy you an outfit for the party.'

'I don't like wearing dresses.'

'It doesn't have to be a dress,' he stressed. Again. She'd been happy enough about going to the celebration party he was throwing until he'd mentioned the dress code and she'd become mutinous. He would never understand her. 'Just something that isn't jeans.'

'I feel comfortable in jeans.'

'Yes, but you won't feel comfortable if you're the only one wearing them. Everyone's dressing up.'

Her eyes narrowed and her lips pursed. 'Just don't expect me to wear heels. Not going to happen.'

'Fine.'

'Good. Can we get food now?'

Lacing his fingers through hers, Emiliano led her out of the store. The sun had risen, spring warmth filling the busy Buenos Aires streets. A short walk later and they were shown to an outside table at a chic restaurant that sold a mean *submarino*, a milk drink served with a chunk of chocolate he just knew Becky would love, especially as she'd vowed to only have one coffee a day for the duration of the pregnancy. His instinct on this was correct and he watched her stir the chocolate into the hot milk with an enchanted smile at this small pleasure.

While they waited for their food to be brought to them, he set about quizzing her.

'What happened with your mother?'

The enchanted smile fell. 'Can't we just relax for half an hour?'

'It is not relaxing to talk about your mother?'

'No.'

'Why not?'

She scowled. 'Honestly, you really are a bulldozer when you want something.'

'I don't like evasion.'

Her eyes flashed. 'That had better not be a dig.'

'I just find it curious that you've never mentioned you're not on speaking terms with your mother.'

'Seriously?' She leaned forward. 'You know what *I* find curious? That this is a repeat of a conversation we've had before. I work for you for months and you never ask me any personal questions whatsoever, then when you discover new things about me you act all surprised and immediately assume I've been hiding things. You are so cynical!'

'And you're still hiding.'

'I am *not*. I don't like to talk about it because it still hurts.'

'Your mother?'

She nodded and had a sip of her *submarino*. The chocolate must have soothed her for she closed her eyes to savour it and her shoulders loosened. 'We fell out at Christmas.'

'What happened?'

'We had an argument about her new husband and she kicked me out.'

As Emiliano took a moment to digest this, their food was brought to them. He hadn't known her mother had remarried.

He took a bite of his steak baguette before saying, 'What was the argument about?'

She looked away from him with a shrug.

'You remember that night when we spoke about my mother on the porch?'

Her eyes flickered.

'I didn't hold anything back.'

'Yes, you did.'

'I did not.'

'Did too. You wouldn't tell me why you were sacked from the family business.'

'It wasn't relevant to the conversation.'

Her narrowing eyes told him she saw straight through this evasion.

He sighed. 'Look, it's a time in my life that still makes me angry to think of. I never speak about it.'

'Did it involve a woman?'

Now his eyes narrowed.

Shaking her head, she dug her spoon into the *provoleta* still bubbling in the skillet it had been served to her in, and blew on the gooey cheese she lifted out. He'd learned these past few days that Becky's savoury tooth was as big as her sweet tooth.

'You have big trust issues when it comes to women,' she observed, before popping the spoon into her mouth.

'So would you if you had a mother like mine.'

'Nice evasion.'

'I must have learned it from you.'

Their eyes clashed and then, in an instant, her taut features loosened at the same moment he felt the tightness in his chest loosen and they both started laughing.

Emiliano caught hold of her hand and brought it to his lips. 'Just wait until I get you home.'

'Ooh, what are you going to do to me?'

'I'm going to make love to you for so long you won't be able to walk for a week.'

'Promises, promises,' she teased with a gleam in her eyes. Her foot found his calf and gently rubbed against it.

Still smiling, she dipped her rustic bread into her *provoleta* and had a bite that was pure provocation.

'You, *bomboncita*, could drive a saint to madness.'

'Just as well you're not a saint then.'

CHAPTER TEN

EMILIANO WAS AS good as his word. Within minutes of them returning to the ranch he'd locked his bedroom door, stripped her naked and made love to her for so long she doubted she'd be able to walk for a month. It was glorious.

Utterly sated, she dozed while he went off to exercise the dogs, only stirring when he returned to the room and slipped back into bed to make love to her all over again.

When she finally left the bed to shower, she couldn't help but giggle to feel the delicious lethargy in her limbs.

Back in the bedroom, wrapped in Emiliano's way too big robe, which she'd claimed for her own, she was thrilled to see he'd had dinner brought to them.

He grinned. 'I thought it saved us having to get dressed.'

'I like your thinking.'

After they'd eaten a great dish of *carbonada* each, an Argentinian beef stew that had a wonderful sweetness to it, Emiliano put the television on and stretched out on the sofa. Becky lay beside him, her back against his torso, bottom resting against his groin, and he wrapped his arms tightly around her.

Although a tactile person, he'd never been a man for cuddling. It was one of the many intimacies he'd chosen to avoid and he found it a little alarming how good it felt to lie like this, not speaking, not making love, simply holding each other. He decided it was best not to ponder on this.

When the documentary ended he kissed the top of her head. She sighed and stretched her back.

'I thought you'd fallen asleep,' he murmured.

'Just thinking.'

'About?'

'Us. The baby. My parents. How we can avoid the mistakes they made.'

'Ready to tell me about it?'

She sighed again and wriggled onto her back. 'It wasn't that I didn't want to tell you, just that

I didn't want to do it in public. It's still pretty raw for me.'

He adjusted himself so he could look at her face more clearly while still keeping his body pressed against hers. 'Was their divorce recent?'

'The divorce itself was finalised a year ago but the separation happened when I left for university. Literally, I left on the Saturday and Mum kicked Dad out on the Sunday. She'd been waiting for me to "flee the nest", as she put it.'

'Did you say they married because she got pregnant with you?'

She nodded. 'They were very young. Mum was nineteen; Dad was twenty.'

'My mum was only twenty when she had me. But they were already married.'

She smiled and brushed a thumb against his mouth. 'Mine should have stayed single. They spent my entire childhood arguing. Not passionate arguments or anything like that, but constant cold sniping at each other.'

'How were they with you?'

'Great. Very loving and supportive in everything I did. They just hated each other. They were like children taking constant pot-shots at each other. Mum told me after that she'd known since I was a toddler that the minute I was old enough to cope and understand, she would end the marriage.'

'Was it a relief for you when it ended?'

'It would have been if they'd stayed the same people, but they both changed. The only thing that didn't change was the bickering—if anything, the separation made them worse. They fought about everything, right down to the koi carp in the garden pond. That's why the divorce took so long to go through. In the end, the courts decided how the marital assets were split and neither of them was happy about it so it must have been the right judgement. Mum got the house, half their savings and half Dad's pension. Dad got the business.'

'Catering, wasn't it?'

'Event catering. He built it from nothing and it became very successful, which was just as well as the pair of them spent a fortune on lawyers' fees. The divorce was rubber-stamped a year ago and Mum remarried pretty much immediately. Dad sold the business and bought himself a motorbike to travel around Europe.

He says he's recapturing his lost youth. He video calls every month or so. You should see him; he's grown his hair and a beard and has loads of young women falling over him. Amazing what a powerful bike and a wallet stuffed with cash does to a man's sex appeal. He's now planning to travel America so I've no idea when I'll see him again.'

'That must be rough.'

'It is.' A flash of real pain rang from her eyes. 'I miss him.'

'What happened with your stepfather?'

Her features visibly tightened at the mention of him. 'Ruddy gold-digging con-artist.'

Emiliano propped himself on an elbow to study her face even more closely. His nightmare with Adriana had made gold-digging con-artists a specialist subject for him. 'Really?'

'He's a slimy twenty-seven-year-old personal trainer who usually dates hot young women. Mum hired him a couple of years ago. He moved in within weeks of them getting together and they married a month after the divorce was finalised.'

'Why do you think he's a gold-digger?' he

asked carefully, thinking that until he'd met Becky his own type had been blonde, stick-thin models and socialites with bust sizes higher than their IQs. 'I understand why her marrying someone your age would make you feel uncomfortable but the age gap between them is less than the one between Celeste and my father—my adoptive father, I mean—and tastes change. Is it because your mother is the older party?'

'I'd already got used to her having lovers my age. She put me in the annexe rather than let me move back into the main house as she said I needed privacy, but really it was to keep me out of sight and stop me cramping her style when her current lover was around. Anthony was the first one she really fell for. If I thought he was genuine I wouldn't care, but I've seen first-hand what a sly, spoilt, manipulative narcissist he is. He's got her wrapped around his finger. He hasn't worked a day since they married, but she's bought him a sports car, a wardrobe of designer clothes and had a gym installed for him. All he has to do is look at something and he gets it, and then the bastard thought he could have me too.'

A trickle of ice ran down his spine. 'What happened?'

Her chin jutted and her lips tightened before she answered. 'I'd run out of coffee so popped into the house to borrow some. I didn't know Mum had gone food shopping for the Christmas party they were hosting. The creep pinned me to the kitchen wall and said he'd seen me looking at him…' her face contorted with distaste '…and knew that I wanted him. Then he stuck his tongue down my throat and groped me.'

The trickle of ice turned into a sea that spread through his veins. 'Did he hurt you?'

Green eyes flashed with rage. 'My reflexes worked too well for that. I kneed him right where it hurts the most.'

'Good,' he said grimly although he was already thinking ahead to ways he could exact proper retribution. 'And then what happened?'

'I locked myself in the annexe until Mum got back but I was so upset and angry that I could hardly speak to tell her. Anthony was as cool as a cucumber and denied everything. He said I was jealous and trying to split them up because I wanted him for myself. She believed him and kicked me out right there and then.'

For a moment Emiliano couldn't speak. It was as if a hand had plunged through his ribcage, grabbed hold of his heart and twisted it.

'I haven't spoken to her since. She won't answer my calls or messages. I'm dead to her.'

To his horror, two fat tears spilled from her eyes.

'Have you told her about the baby?' he asked gently. 'That might be the bridge you two need to rebuild things.'

'I've been too scared.' She squeezed her eyes shut and pinched her nose. 'What if she ignores it like she's ignored all the other messages? I've begged her over and over to talk and I get nothing back. I don't know how I'd cope if she were to reject our baby too.'

Not saying a word, Emiliano lay back down and pulled her to him, wrapping his arms tightly around her and stroking her hair as she cried into his chest.

For Becky, his silent comfort spoke more than any meaningless words could say. All this time, she'd believed she was coping but she saw now that she'd only buried the pain out of reach.

Within weeks of kicking Becky's father out her mum had hooked up with her first young lover. Becky remembered being homesick and deciding to visit, only to have her mum send her back as she had a weekend of partying planned. Hurt—*devastated*—and at a loss at how to handle it, Becky had thrown herself into her studies. She'd tried to understand her mum's newfound enthusiasm for younger men, tried to pretend the maternal love she'd always taken for granted wasn't being tainted by suspicion from a mother who'd stopped looking at her as a daughter and begun seeing her as a rival. And then that horrendous day had come; her mum shrieking at her like a harpy, accusing Becky of jealousy and spite while her new husband watched with that hateful smirk…

Estranged from her mother, her father thousands of miles away, she'd thrown herself into her studies with a vengeance, completing her doctorate in record time, working her brain harder than she'd ever done until she burnt herself out. But even then she hadn't paused long enough to think and certainly not long enough to feel. She'd thrown herself into the hospitality work and then the work for Emiliano, filling the months before starting her new job. Anything rather than face up to the reality that she was truly alone.

Who would have believed, she thought in wonder as the tears dried up, that selfish, arrogant Emiliano Delgado would be the one she would finally open up to and confide in? And who would have believed him capable of listening so well and giving such tender comfort?

There were a lot of things she would never have believed about him. The spoilt playboy was only one facet of the man and, she was coming to believe, only the shiny surface of him. Beneath it, he was a man capable of great kindness and empathy.

'Where did you go after you left?' he asked quietly once all the tears had been purged.

'I moved into Dad's mobile home. He bought it when Mum kicked him out. He'd already gone off on his bike trip by then.'

'Why didn't you go to another family member or a friend?'

'The rest of my family live by the coast a hundred miles away—my parents moved to the

Midlands when they married. As for friends...'
She shrugged and tried to sound nonchalant. 'I
didn't really have anyone I was close enough
with to ask.'

He was silent for a moment. 'What happens
when the baby comes? Will you have anyone
close by to help?'

'No,' she admitted with a sigh.

'So when you go back to England you're not
going to have any emotional support?'

Becky closed her eyes and held back fresh
tears at his accuracy. She'd done enough crying for one day. 'I'll cope.'

'If you marry me you won't have to cope.
We can do it together.'

'Not this again?' She wriggled out of his hold
and rolled onto her back.

'There is no reason our marriage would be
like your parents'.'

'But we'd be doing it for the wrong reasons,
the same as they did.'

'And what are the right reasons?'

'Love, fidelity and commitment,' she said in
as strong a voice as she could manage. 'None
of which you can offer me.'

He stared straight into her eyes. 'If we marry, you will have my commitment as a husband.'

'But no guarantee of fidelity.' She couldn't bring herself to mention love again, not when her heart had started thumping so erratically. 'I would have to give up the career I've dedicated my life to before I've even started while you get to continue yours as if nothing's changed, except you'd have a wife and baby tagging along.'

He breathed heavily through the tense silence that developed. 'You do realise I want to be a father to our child?'

'Yes, I do know that and I want it too.'

'Then tell me how it'll work if you're living with it on the other side of the world from me? I never knew my real father and the man who adopted me never wanted me. I don't want that for my child. My real father had no choice about raising me. God took that choice from him but I do have that choice and I'm going to take it. I want our child to know they're loved and wanted by both their parents.'

'You have a home in England. You could always base yourself there. It's only twenty miles from where I'll be working...' She let her words hang and held her breath.

'That's impossible,' he said shortly, shifting upright.

'Why?'

'You know why. I move from country to country with the polo seasons and on top of that I have my stables around the world and—'

'I know the extent of your empire,' she interrupted wearily. 'I know how busy your life is, and we can argue all night over whose job should take priority and maybe we'd even come to an agreement, but one thing we won't reach agreement on is marriage. You can be as involved in our child's upbringing as you want but I'm sorry, I'm not going to throw away my career so I can stand on the sidelines cheering you on like one of your fawning groupies and lose my career and independence for someone who can't be faithful. I've lost too much already.'

'You don't know that I won't be faithful.'

'And neither do you.'

'I know I would never do anything to hurt or humiliate you. While we are together I am yours alone.'

Tightening the robe around her waist, Becky sat up and cupped his clenched jaw in her hands and looked him in the eye. 'Then you can't blame me for refusing to marry you or uprooting my life for you. Marriage should be a lifetime commitment. When you tell me you'll be faithful only for as long as we're together, that proves to me that you don't trust yourself to sustain it for a lifetime.'

At the darkening of his features, she sighed and pressed a kiss to his taut lips. 'It's still early days for us. We're still getting to know each other. We both want to make it work as best we can. Let that be enough.'

The darkness firing from his clear brown eyes softened. 'Marriage is the only thing that will be enough for me, *bomboncita*. But you are right. It's still early days for us. I have plenty of time to change your mind.'

Then, before she could refute his impossible arrogance, he'd pulled her into a kiss of such seductive passion that any protest melted under its heat.

Becky sat well back from the action on the polo field. The dogs were gazing at her with begging eyes for titbits of the picnic food she'd brought along. The ground beneath her bottom shook as eight ponies and riders thundered past.

Today was the Delgado team's first practice of the Argentine season. From the noise, speed and aggression taking place on the field, the players were approaching it as if it were a competition game. As had been the case from the first game she'd watched, she only had eyes for Emiliano. He just looked so magnificent on the sleek Arabian horse—sorry, pony!—he was currently charging around on, and for a moment she visualised him as a warrior from bygone days leading the cavalry into war. If he'd been around in those bygone times, she had no doubt he would have been a natural warrior, leading from the front and commanding respect wherever he went.

She watched him now, riding furiously as he chased the comparatively tiny ball up the field, his mallet aimed and ready to strike, a member of the opposing team cantering alongside preparing to ride him off, but for the first time the tingles she usually experienced seeing his raw power in action were absent. For the first time, a nugget of fear had clutched at her heart and that fear was spreading.

The strictly enforced rules of polo were designed for the horses' safety. She remembered a wife from an opposing team telling her that so long as the riders were properly taught and maintained their discipline the dangers were minimal.

For the first time Becky truly comprehended that minimal didn't mean zero. Maybe it was the pregnancy working its hormonal magic on her but suddenly all she could see were the potential dangers of this chaotically exhilarating game.

Emiliano's birth father had been a polo player. He'd died in a freak horse accident.

There was a great roar from the other spectators—only a couple of dozen or so stable staff, but loud enough to be mistaken for a dozen rowdy stag parties—and when she opened her eyes she hadn't realised she'd closed she saw Emiliano had scored. There was little time to celebrate as one of the umpires signalled the end of the chukka and they all trooped off the field to change their ponies and Becky was able to refill lungs that had barely snatched a breath in seven minutes. When Emiliano rode past her, every female eye in the vicinity glued to him, and winked, she had to force her lips and cheeks to perform a smile but her heart was thundering as hard as the horses' hooves.

Terrified as to why she should feel so frightened, she pulled her phone out of her pocket, hoping to have received another work email to distract her. They'd been coming thick and fast in recent days, preparing her for when she started. Right then, any kind of email would be welcome but her inbox was empty.

This must be why normal people used social media. It was easier to hide away from your thoughts with visual distractions.

The skills she'd adopted to distract herself from unwelcome thoughts were dismantling. Her fears had grown too great, crowding a head too full to cope. And now she had another to add to them. Emiliano being hurt. More than a fear. A poker of ice freezing her insides.

Impulse had her pressing her mum's contact details and selecting the call button. It rang three times before going to voicemail.

Becky closed her eyes and listened to her mum's chirpy voice telling her to leave a message.

'Hi, Mum… It's me. Please call me. I miss you. I… I have something to tell you. It's important. Please. I don't want to tell you in a message. Call me back, *please*… I love you.'

When she disconnected the call, Rufus and Barney both had their heads on her lap and were gazing at her dolefully.

She rubbed both their heads and blinked back the threatening tears. 'At least you two love me,' she whispered, and wished Emiliano's face didn't immediately float through her mind at the mention of the word love.

CHAPTER ELEVEN

BECKY CHECKED HER appearance for the hundredth time before leaving the room. Excitement laced her belly. She felt as if she could cha-cha down the wide corridors.

Emiliano had been so busy preparing for the forthcoming Argentine polo season that the only time they'd spent alone together in recent days had been in the bedroom. That morning, when he'd dragged himself out of bed after making love to her, he'd winked and told her he'd be taking her out for dinner that night.

She'd spent the day smiling at the irony that their first date should take place weeks after the conception of their child and refusing to think that the countdown to her return to England was speeding up. Only ten days left.

She'd deliberated for ages over what to wear. Their shopping trip for a dress for the party he was hosting—she couldn't believe that was happening in two days; time really was flying by—had seen her wardrobe mushroom by far more than a single dress. She'd returned from that shopping trip to find box upon box of beautiful clothing, all of which had fitted perfectly and all of which suited her, laid out in their bedroom.

The personal shopper who'd helped her find the party dress had obviously been much busier than she'd credited, Emiliano every bit as sneaky and as wholeheartedly generous as she already knew he could be.

For their meal out, she'd eventually settled on a knee-length silver shift dress that sparkled under the movement of light and a pair of flat black ankle boots, and she hurried out of the room before she could change her mind again. She'd dithered so much about it, she wouldn't be surprised to find the sun had risen in the intervening period never mind set.

The look on Emiliano's face when she stepped into the living room made all the dilly-dallying worthwhile. He whistled, the gleam in his eyes making her blush.

'You look good enough to eat,' he murmured in an undertone when he reached her, setting off her second blush in as many seconds.

He could talk, she thought dizzily as she slipped her hand in his. The man could wear sackcloth and she'd still feel faint with longing. Seeing him dressed in navy trousers and a black shirt that stretched across his lean yet muscular body like a caress, his spicy cologne coiling into her airways, she could, quite frankly, eat him alive.

The dogs left in Paula's care for the evening, they left the ranch in the waiting car.

The driver dropped them off at a corner of a huge plaza in Luján province and a quick stroll later they were inside a large, dark restaurant with a vibe that lent itself to intimacy despite the open kitchen where chefs could be seen working as in a hive over wall-length griddles.

A flustered waitress who clearly recognised Emiliano led them to a small round table near the corner of the room, close to a small stage and an even smaller dance floor. Just off the side of the stage was a tiny round table with a glass of red wine in the centre.

'Does this place do entertainment?' Becky asked.

He winked. 'Wait and see.'

Their table was so small that there was no

way to sit comfortably without their legs brushing, which was fine by Becky. Any excuse to touch Emiliano was fine by her, and she knew it was the same for him. How long this passion could be sustained was something she now refused to think about. She might have refused marriage but she'd committed herself to him. They had only ten days left until she returned to England and she didn't want to waste them worrying about things beyond her control.

The waitress returned with their drinks. 'Ready to order?' she asked breathlessly, making gooey eyes at Emiliano.

Smothering the urge to throw her mocktail in the waitress's face, Becky smiled brightly and got the waitress's attention. 'I would like the ham and cheese *empanadas* to start, then the two-hundred-and-fifty-gram sirloin with fries and salad and Portobello mushrooms on the side.'

She caught the amusement on Emiliano's face before he gave his own order.

Alone again, he leaned forward. 'Do I detect jealousy, *bomboncita*?'

'Not at all,' she lied airily. 'I just think it's

mean to openly make eyes and flirt with someone who's clearly taken.'

He stroked her hand and murmured, 'So long
as you know I only have eyes for you.'

'I know.' She smiled, and swallowed back
the pang she always felt when she wondered
how long that exclusivity would last.

He opened his mouth but whatever he'd been
about to say was cut off by the buzzing of his
phone.

'I'll turn it off,' he said apologetically, then
his eyes narrowed as he saw who'd messaged
him. 'Sorry, let me read this. It's from Damián.'

He read quickly. A wide smile spread across
his face.

'Good news?'

He nodded. 'Celeste's been arrested.' He put
the phone back in his jacket pocket. 'I know
she'll be released soon but at least the press
were there to witness her humiliation. I can
celebrate that.' He raised his glass, smiled
again and took a large drink.

'You seem remarkably serene about your
mother being a killer,' she remarked, thinking back to the night he'd turned up at her door
in such torment.

Emiliano laughed. 'Not serene, *bomboncita*. Accepting. I admit it was a shock when I first learned what she'd done.' And Becky was the only person in the world who knew how deeply it had affected him. 'But after it sank in, it was no surprise. I've always known she's capable of anything.'

'But *murder*?'

'Celeste's world revolves around Celeste. She doesn't do anything that isn't for her own benefit. Take Damián's conception. When she agreed to marry Eduardo, she agreed to give him a blood heir. As soon as that agreement was fulfilled, she got herself sterilised.'

He laughed at the disbelieving expression on Becky's face. 'You can't be surprised that she has no maternal instincts. She upheld her side of the agreement and gave Eduardo a child, Damián, then washed her hands of the task of actually raising either of us. Being a hands-on mother was *not* part of their agreement.'

'You sound as if you admire her,' she said with a furrowed brow.

'There was an honesty to their marriage I always admired,' he mused. 'They both knew where they stood. No lies.'

'That must be where you get your honesty from,' Becky said. That was one thing about Emiliano; he was always honest.

He grinned. 'As long as that's the only trait I inherited from her, I can live with that. But the more I think about her killing him, the more convinced I am that she felt my father had not upheld his end of their deal. She'd believed she would always have involvement in the Delgado Group. Giving control to Damián pushed her out of the sphere of influence and she refused to accept it. She is not a woman willing to accept no as an answer to anything.'

Another trait he'd inherited from her, Becky thought, but chose not to vocalise it.

'Do you still want her to be involved in your life?'

'No,' he said without hesitation. 'She's poison. Literally. If anything, knowing I have a legitimate reason to cut her from my life is a relief. I see now that I was only ever a pawn she used for her own ends. Even when she talked me into working for the Delgado Group, it was for her benefit, not mine—she assumed I would spy on Damián for her.'

'Did you?'

'No. I told her to do her own dirty work.'

The breathless waitress brought their first course to them and for a while they were both too busy eating to talk. Once the course had been cleared and fresh drinks given to them, Emiliano took her hand and pressed a kiss to her fingers. 'No more family talk tonight, okay? Let's just enjoy the evening and each other's company.'

'That sounds good to me,' she agreed softly. Becky always enjoyed his company, even during the times when she could throttle him.

She had another drink of her mocktail. The rush of feelings she had simply being with Emiliano meant she didn't miss drinking alcohol. Being with him felt very much like being drunk.

When their main courses were brought to them, she inhaled the wonderful scents and cut into her juicy steak. The knife sank through the meat as if it were softened butter. She popped her fork into her mouth and for the breath of a moment forgot everything as her mouth filled with heaven.

Emiliano cut into his ribeye with the same unabashed appreciation. When he looked at her after taking his first huge bite, something in her belly moved, like an intense tug, a fist clenching simultaneously in her chest.

Was this what her mother had experienced with Anthony? With all the others that had come before him? Were these the heady feelings that had seen her believe the worst of her only child and cut her from her life?

But they'd agreed no more family talk so she pushed thoughts of her mother aside and relaxed into a conversation about the dogs, the subject they'd first bonded over all that time ago.

Becky had just taken the last spoonful of her ice cream dessert when a group of musicians suddenly appeared in the darkly lit room and climbed the three steps onto the stage beside them. 'Is there going to be live music?'

He drained his glass of wine and smiled knowingly.

Pushing her empty bowl to one side, she shifted her chair next to Emiliano's for a better view and laced her fingers through his.

She nodded at a man with what looked like an accordion in his arms. 'Do you know what that is?'

'It's a bandoneon. A type of concertina.'

Beside the bandoneon player, three violinists, a cellist and a guitarist were tuning their instruments. A flautist shuffled his chair to his preferred position.

Another round of drinks was brought to their table and then the restaurant's already dim lights faded further, the candles on the tables casting their fellow diners into silhouettes. The bandoneon player struck his first notes and the band began to play. The music was dark and sensuous, with sharp staccatos and dreamy sections pitched perfectly.

A spotlight appeared on the dance floor and a woman in a tight-fitting black dress with a slit all the way up to her hip appeared. She walked to the small round table on the side of the stage and, to the sound of the solo cellist, took a sip from the glass of wine.

A man wearing a shiny black suit and fedora approached her and put a hand to her shoulder. He spun her round to face him in one graceful movement.

Becky gasped and tightened her hold on Emiliano's fingers. He squeezed back, enjoying the way her eyes stayed glued on the sinuous dance unfolding before them. The hand not holding his absently strummed on the table in time to the music. His gaze roved between the dancers, whose bodies seemed to move as one while their legs flicked and clicked around each other in a blur, and the beautiful, incredibly sexy woman beside him.

She shifted in her seat and pressed closer to him. Her fragrant scent unleashed and dived into his senses. Heat, never far away when he was with Becky, released in a tidal wave to grab him by the throat and suddenly Emiliano found himself enveloped in a heavy cloud of desire but with a weight in his chest that made it impossible to breathe or move.

For all its sensuousness, the Argentine Tango, at its essence, was a lament to lost love. Watching the desperate passion unfold before him… For a moment Emiliano felt as if he was watching a prophecy.

He blinked the unsettling thought away and released his hold on Becky's hand so he could wrap his arm around her.

Eyes not leaving the dancers, she leaned into him, her hand automatically groping for his.

Fingers laced through hers, the unsettling melancholy crept back on him. Only another ten days until she flew back to England.

He tried to find his usual positive mind-set, reminding himself of the progress he'd made with her. They'd worked the dates out and they were in his favour. Becky would start her maternity leave at around the same time as the US polo season finished. He would fly straight back to the UK and she would move into his home there, which would give them around a month to create a nursery for their baby in one of the spare rooms before its birth. He'd finally got her agreement that when she moved into his UK home it would be permanent. In the meantime, she had agreed to fly out to Argentina to spend Christmas with him. He would fly over to England whenever practicable.

Many conversations with diaries and schedules and a good deal of willingness had seen them find common ground but the one issue he couldn't budge her on was marriage. It had reached the stage where if he brought the subject up she would walk out of the room rather than discuss it.

He knew what she was waiting for. What was stopping him from saying the words?

Was it the control he was as guilty as the rest of the Delgados for craving?

Fear?

He didn't know and right then he didn't care. Screw stealth. He'd proven himself useless at it. There was only one way to get Becky's agreement to marry him.

'If you marry me, I promise to be faithful for the rest of our lives,' he murmured. 'I will make that promise to you.'

She stiffened and tilted her head to stare at him with wide eyes. 'Is it a promise you can keep?'

'If that's the promise I need to make for you to agree, then I will make it and I will keep it, however hard it may be. I will do that for you.' He stroked her cheek and rubbed his nose to hers. 'Don't answer me now. Think seriously about it. Give me your answer after the party. If the answer's no then I will never mention marriage again. I give you my word.'

A voice whispered in his head that if her answer was no, then he would perform a lament of his own…

* * *

Emiliano brought Diggity to a stop and watched the army of people coordinate perfectly to heave the marquee upright. Rows of large vans were parked close by, filled with tables and chairs, and in the distance catering vans approached. In a few hours, the vans would be gone and the marquee would be ready for the two hundred or so people coming to celebrate the end of a successful English polo season and the beginning of the Argentine one. He wondered if they'd be better behaved than they'd been at the last party he'd thrown, at the end of the US season at his home in Palm Springs. Very doubtful, he thought with a wry smile, before tapping his ankle into Diggity's flank and setting off again, this time back to the stables.

Spirits were high when he returned. The practice sessions the team had had for the new season were proving their worth. Nicky, the new player he'd poached from a rival team, was fitting in smoothly, his horses even more so. Emiliano's own horses had recovered well from the journey from England.

He should be raring for the new season to start but his spirits were flat. Becky hadn't mentioned his latest proposal but he knew she was considering it. She hadn't dismissed it out of hand. He wanted to take that as a good sign, but with Becky...

He sighed. He could never take her thoughts or actions for granted.

Feeling too out of sorts to mix with people, he rode back out of the stables to one of his vast open fields at a canter. Riding his beasts at speed was one of life's greatest joys. One of Emiliano's biggest regrets was being born a foot too tall to be a jockey. He would have loved racing; coaxing his horse past all the others, leaving rivals in his wake and smashing past the finish line. Truth was, he loved winning. On a horse, he was invincible. He had a natural affinity with the creatures, which had allowed him to dominate the polo scene for so many years. Before he retired he wanted a year when his team, with him at the helm, won every major cup competition in England, Argentina and the US. He'd won them all individually but never the clean sweep. This year he'd already won the most prestigious English one and it had been a bitter realisation that he couldn't send a cutting of himself holding the trophy aloft to his father.

He'd done that for the past decade. While he'd stopped caring what his adoptive father or anyone else thought of him, whatever success he'd had, he'd made sure Eduardo had known. His three Argentine Open cups had all been couriered to him.

But now Eduardo, the man who'd adopted him then thrown him aside as if he were dirt, was dead and, for the first time, Emiliano could acknowledge the hunger that had driven him to succeed for so long had dimmed.

When had that happened? Eduardo had been dead for months before the English season started, and he'd approached that with his usual gusto.

He didn't know what was wrong with him, only that something was. It was inside him. Something off-kilter. Something that felt very much like fear.

CHAPTER TWELVE

BECKY CAME OUT of the woods with the dogs and found the sun beaming down. Emiliano would be happy. He'd been concerned about the weather changing for the evening's party but, for the moment, there was not a puff of cloud marring the vast blue skies above. She didn't want to think about the autumnal weather she'd be flying back to when she returned to England. She should be there already, settling into her rented flat and preparing for her new job which started in exactly eight days.

Emiliano's promise of fidelity if she married him played constantly in her mind. A huge part of her wanted to say yes. So long as he respected her career, they could make it work. Maintaining a long-distance marriage wouldn't be easy but they'd already reached agreement on so much. They could make it work.

So what was stopping her from saying yes?

She was mere paces away from the ranch when her phone vibrated. Snatching it out of her pocket, her heart leapt to see her mother had finally messaged her back.

Hands shaking, she walked up the steps and sat on the swing chair.

And then she read it and the hope that had clutched her heart turned to despair. A whole week she'd prayed for a response. Seven whole days. And this was what she received?

A burst of fury suddenly blazed through her veins and, fingers working of their own accord, she typed out a response and pressed send before she had time to think about it. Her response consisted of two words: *I'm pregnant.*

Another burst of fury crashed through her at her stupidity in sending the message and, in a fit of pique, she hurled the phone through the air as hard as she could.

Emiliano, who'd returned to the ranch for food, had seen Becky, head bowed over her phone, clearly too caught up in whatever she was dealing with to notice his approach.

Crouching down to pick up the offending phone, which had landed only a foot from him, he took another two steps closer before she finally noticed him. He swiftly put his hands in the air. 'Whatever it is, I didn't do it.'

Her taut red, angry face softened to see him. A tiny splutter of laughter fell from her lips.

'Sorry,' she muttered, 'I didn't see you there.'

'So I gathered. Unless you really did see me and just don't want to admit you have a lousy aim?'

'I have that too.'

He handed her phone back before sitting beside her and taking her hand. 'What's wrong?'

She shrugged.

'Becky?'

'Mum's messaged me.' She took a long breath then swiped at her phone. She brought the message up and handed it to him.

His heart thumped as he read.

I thought I'd made it clear that I will not listen to your lies. Anthony and I are very happy. The last thing we need is for you to inflict more of your jealous spite on us. Get your head out of your books and find yourself a man and STOP trying to steal mine.

'Well, that's me told,' she said with a brave shrug.

'You tried to make contact with her?'

She nodded. 'I left her a message during your first practice session.'

'You never mentioned it.'

She shrugged again. 'I was scared to build my hopes up. Guess I was right.'

'She really thinks you're trying to steal her husband?'

'Looks like it.' She laughed morosely. 'She used to tease me about my reluctance to date. I would bite my tongue to stop myself shouting that the only way I could cope with the loss of my family and with my parents being at war and my mum turning into a cougar overnight was by throwing myself into the books she's now so dismissive of. It would have been easier if they'd split when I was a toddler. I wouldn't have gone from being a loved daughter to a rival. She's infatuated with him.'

Emiliano ran his fingers through his hair. He didn't know if he'd felt worse the other week when she'd bawled her eyes out or now, seeing her so wan and so utterly defeated. At least when she'd cried he'd been able to hold her and comfort her. Now, he just felt useless.

But there was one thing he could do that might help.

'I understand why she chose him over you,' he admitted heavily, and felt her freeze beside him. 'But I need you to understand that, as personal as it feels, it is not about you. It's about her. And one day she will come to her senses.'

She turned her head slowly to him, eyes wide. She gave one large blink.

'The truth will come to her sooner or later. It always does.' Emiliano dragged his hand down his face then leaned forward to rest his elbows on his thighs. 'The reason my time at the Delgado Group ended so badly was because I fell in love with a gold-digging con-artist.'

Becky almost jumped at the unexpected admission. Emiliano had been in *love*...?

'Her name was Adriana. I hired her as my PA. I'd been given control of a major investment fund—I won't bore you with the details but collectively the funds in it were worth tens of billions. I was new to the game and needed assistance from someone already in the industry.

'Adriana had an impeccable résumé...' he looked at her with a faint smile '...one of the reasons I don't bother with them any more. It was love at first sight for both of us. She was beautiful and clever and she played me like a pro. I wanted to go public but she always resisted, which just added to her allure. I thought she wanted to keep it special between us but she was protecting herself because, while I was imagining our future, she was hacking into my work accounts and performing a heist of such nerve that I admit to having a grudging respect for it.'

'What did she do?' Becky breathed, half afraid to hear.

'She syphoned exactly four hundred and ninety-eight million dollars from the accounts I had control of. She did it so subtly that it took weeks for the theft to be discovered but by then it was too late—she'd gone too. We'd spent a weekend together and I swear I had no idea anything was up. She went home on the Sunday evening, kissed me goodbye as normal and that was the last I saw her. When she didn't turn up for work I was out of my mind with worry. I went to her apartment and it was empty. She'd disappeared overnight. It took weeks for me to learn she'd left with half a billion dollars, all neatly deposited into an off-shore tax haven I couldn't touch.'

'Oh, my God,' she whispered.

'I learned much later that I wasn't her first victim. She'd spent a year in an English prison for defrauding two companies. I'm sure there're others.'

'So what happened? Was she arrested?'

His eyes locked back onto hers. 'You're the first person I've told this story to.'

She just stared at him.

'I hired some private detectives to find her but I didn't give them reasons. They tracked her to a private island in the Caribbean in a territory with no extradition treaties. It's a criminals' paradise. She's still there, living the high life on stolen money…albeit surrounded by criminals. And she knows that I know where she is. I made sure of that. I have people watching her. She will never leave. She's too frightened of the consequences.'

She was almost afraid to ask. 'What will they be?'

'I've a file as thick as my arm with the trail she left. There's enough evidence in it to have her sent down for twenty years.'

Swallowing back the nausea churning in her belly and blinking away the blurring in her eyes, Becky forced her thoughts away from Emiliano being in love. 'So you didn't tell your family about it?'

He sighed and rubbed the nape of his neck. 'When the losses were discovered, their first assumption was that I'd messed up. I was still trying to unravel the trail Adriana had left. I knew she'd had something to do with it but at that point I had no proof. I would have enlisted their help but all they did was shout and rail at me, assuming I was at fault. Celeste had convinced them to hire me—she'd damn well convinced me to work for them too—and for them this was confirmation that I should never have been given a chance. I was booted out and paid off to keep quiet. They couldn't afford for it to come out that half a billion of their clients' monies had disappeared.'

'They kept it a secret?' she asked in astonishment.

'As far as I know, they paid the funds back from their private accounts. I would have felt guilty for that but, as far as I was concerned, they could go to hell.' His smile was so cold she shivered. 'It just proved they'd never trusted me and that they'd been waiting for me to mess up. So screw them. I'd worked my backside off in an environment I hated and I think part of me did it because deep down I craved their approval. I wanted them to accept me as one of them. My mistake for trusting them when I should have known better. Never trust anything that walks on two feet.'

She couldn't think of a single thing to say. It was too much. The figures he'd mentioned—half a billion dollars!—the way his family had automatically assumed the worst of him and the cold war that had erupted in the Delgado family because of it...

And still, with all that racing through her head, the most shocking admission was that Emiliano had once been in love.

'I tell you this to give you hope,' Emiliano said quietly, although there was a part of him that thought Becky's mother should join Adriana in hell for the way she'd treated her daughter. But Becky loved her. She was pregnant and needed her mother. 'Love makes fools of us. It blinds us. And then one day you open your eyes and you can see again. Your mother's eyes will open to the truth and when they do she will need you. Keep the door open for her and she will come back to you...but when she does, resist the temptation to say *I told you so*,' he added with a rueful smile. 'She will already know.'

Her lips pulled in and she took a long inhalation as she considered his words. 'I hope you're right.'

'I am.'

She gave a tiny snigger which lightened the weight compressing his chest at making an admission he, in his pride, had vowed to never share with anyone. Then her eyes met his and the brief flare of amusement in them dimmed. 'I'm sorry you had to go through that alone.'

He grimaced. 'It was the worst time of my life. I'd been made a fool of. My ego smashed. I still don't know if I felt worse over Adriana's theft or my family's reaction to it. Their reaction would have been the same if I'd told them the truth, that the money had been lost through theft and not negligence. They would have blamed me for not listening to their warnings about gold-diggers.' He blew out a long puff of air. 'I hated the lot of them.'

'And now?'

He considered this. 'My father is dead. Our differences will never be resolved. I could blame Celeste for stealing that opportunity from us but I would never have taken it. He never loved me and nothing I did or said could have changed that. But I still have my brother and, as much as the rage at his treatment still bites me, I know I have to take my share of the blame where he's concerned. Why give someone the benefit of the doubt when he's been consistently horrible to you your entire life?'

'Maybe you should tell him,' she suggested softly. 'Put the past to bed once and for all.'

He rubbed the nape of his neck more vigorously. It was one thing admitting his blind stupidity to Becky but to do the same with Damián? 'What good will it do to rehash the past?'

'To stop the same mistakes being made in the future. From what you've told me, the pair of you are trying to rebuild your relationship after a lifetime of mutual hatred that your mother instigated. I don't see how you can do that properly if the past still has a hold on you.'

'It doesn't.'

'Doesn't it?'

The scepticism in her voice rankled.

'No,' he stated firmly. 'It doesn't. I have reached that greatly revered state of acceptance. I accept my birth father died before I could talk. I accept my adoptive father hated me. I accept that my mother is a psychopath. And I accept that my issues with my brother, although fed by our mother, were all caused by my jealousy. I know the mistakes I made and I will not repeat them. I never do. I learn from them and then I move on.' He lifted his head and flashed his teeth. 'Just as I did learn something from my time at the Delgado Group other than to never trust anyone.'

'Oh?'

'I learned how to play the stock markets. The minute they kicked me out I put that new knowledge into action. That's what I meant when I told you I used the first ten million to get the business rolling. I invested it. In one month that ten million became fifty million. Everything grew from there.'

The buzzing in Becky's head started up again as she thought about the assets he had: the homes, the jets, the art galleries, the world-class stables across the world, the exorbitant costs of running a polo team that travelled *en masse* with the seasons, never mind his racing and dressage horses… Until that moment, it had never occurred to her that the lifestyle he led and the outrageously high overheads his businesses incurred could not be funded with the income from winning races and competitions and stud fees.

But his Midas touch for creating money wasn't the cause of the buzzing in her head. It was the reiteration of his unwillingness to trust people and, for one long moment, she felt a real stab of hatred for Adriana. Ten years ago she hadn't just stolen money from Emiliano. The knock-on effect had stolen his ability to love and trust.

And it was in that moment that the truth Becky had been denying to herself slapped her in the face.

She loved Emiliano. That was what stopped her from agreeing to marriage. She loved him.

All the protections she'd believed she'd placed around her heart to stop him from having the power to break it had been an illusion.

She'd given him her heart the night he'd sought sanctuary from his demons with her.

'Becky?'

He was staring down at her, brow furrowed. She hadn't noticed him get to his feet.

'Sorry,' she murmured. 'I was miles away.'

Unconvinced, he put a hand on her forehead. 'Are you not feeling well?'

'I'm fine. Just a little tired.' She managed a smile. 'Probably hormones. I'll have a nap and then I'll be rested for the party.'

He studied her with the beautiful clear eyes she'd come to love. 'Shall I bring you something up? Food? Mint tea?'

His evident concern was enough to make her want to weep. 'I'll get something later. But thank you.'

And as she climbed the stairs, aware of his penetrating stare still upon her, her hatred for the faceless Adriana and the whole rotten Delgado family filled her throat with bile.

Between them, they hadn't just stolen Emiliano's money and his ability to love and trust. They'd stolen Becky's future. Because she saw no way she could have forever with him now.

* * *

Emiliano finished his lunch, answered some emails, checked that the caterers who'd set up near the marquee were on schedule, then headed up to check on Becky. He was worried about her. She'd been fine one minute, then her face had drained of colour, almost as if she'd had a shock. He supposed that was how pregnancy worked. It must take up a lot of a woman's energy.

The curtains were drawn, darkening the room to a sepia hue. Becky was curled up under the covers, fast asleep.

He sat on the bed and gently stroked her hair. How damn beautiful was this woman. Every time he looked at her he saw something new that made his heart clench. This time it was a tiny mole on her eyelid, and he resisted the urge to press a kiss to it.

When, he wondered, would his desire for her fade? Would he ever reach the stage where he could walk into a room and see her there and not be filled with the compulsion to devour her whole?

She stirred and mumbled something. He wished he could see her dreams. Read her thoughts. Wished he could use telepathy to input thoughts into her beautiful head that proved he would do his damned best to be a good father and a good husband. Make her take that leap of faith.

Her eyes opened. They locked onto his, an emotion he didn't recognise ringing from them, but one that pierced straight into his chest.

She unfurled a naked arm from under the sheets and hooked it round his neck with a sigh. Their lips met in a kiss so relaxed and soft it felt as if he were drugged. Slowly, the sweet warmth of her breath seeped into his airways, rousing the last of his senses not already awoken to her, and he gently tugged the bedding off her so he could lie beside her.

With the same unhurried energy, together they stripped his clothes off him, kissing and stroking each other with a tender desire that burned his heart as much as his loins.

Their eyes stayed locked together when he entered her, fingers tightly entwined, lips brushing.

He would never get over the sensation of making love to Becky or be able to put into words how different it felt, a difference that couldn't be accounted for by the absence of a condom. Although his desire scorched him, making love to her was far more than about sexual release. It was fundamental, as necessary to him as breathing, the need to touch her and be touched by her.

When they were finally spent, Becky's head on his chest, her body pressed against him, Emiliano closed his eyes and took a deep breath to counter the rising trepidation that she still hadn't given him an answer to his latest proposal.

As alien as patience was to him, he must find some. He'd only told her to wait until after the party to answer him to prove he wasn't the bulldozer she kept accusing him of being. He hadn't actually expected her to make him wait that long. Every hour that passed without her answer felt longer than the last.

CHAPTER THIRTEEN

THE THREE-ACRE PRIVATE back garden of
Emiliano's ranch had been transformed into
a spring wonderland. Music pumped from the
huge marquee taking centre-stage, tables and
chairs beneath the canvas and sprawled across
the lawn. The scent of barbecuing meat filled
the air. One thing Becky had learned during
her time in Argentina was that every day was
a potential barbecue day.

The back doors of the ranch had been left
open too, Emiliano being a generous host who
never stood on ceremony when it came to en-
tertaining. For those with children—every
employee was invited to bring their family—
beds were available if naps or downtime was
needed, and specially employed babysitters
were on site so the parents could continue partying. Those who didn't live in the staff quarters, including his polo team and all their staff,
were welcome to stay the night.

Within two hours of it all starting, Becky had decided this was the best party she'd ever been to. It wasn't just the copious amounts of food available or the even more copious amount of drink—she, of course, stuck to soft drinks— keeping everyone refreshed and in high spirits, but the atmosphere in general. She was determined not to let her aching heart spoil things for Emiliano or anyone. The Delgado team and all the supporting staff had earned this night.

Seeing people she normally only saw in jodhpurs or jeans strutting around in pretty dresses and tieless suits made her glad Emiliano had talked her into buying a proper party outfit. Being on the receiving end of many admiring looks, she felt herself blossom like the pink Chinese flowers imprinted on her white dress. She was glad too that he'd convinced her to buy a pair of dusky pink heels to complement it. Compared to some of the women tottering around on heels that should really be called stilts, hers were nothing, but the extra two inches made her feel more elegant than she'd ever felt in her life. Now all she had to do was learn to walk in them!

Even the weather was holding. There were

some pretty ominous-looking clouds in the distance, but to her untrained eye they seemed far enough away that they wouldn't disrupt the party any time soon.

'Coming to dance?' Louise asked as she joined her, clutching a cocktail.

Becky laughed. 'I can't dance.'

'Nor can anyone else.' Sliding her arm through Becky's, Louise bore her off as if they were friends. Which, Becky thought with a little burst of happiness, perhaps they were.

About to enter the marquee, she caught sight of Emiliano impressing a group of small children with his juggling skills. It impressed Becky too. She couldn't juggle one ball never mind three.

He caught her eye, winked and magically produced a fourth ball to juggle with. The children clapped manically.

Emiliano's impromptu performance finished with, he bowed to his audience and followed Becky into the marquee, promising the children trailing after him that he would perform again after he'd had a break.

Helping himself to a beer from the bar inside the marquee, he propped himself on a stool and watched Becky dance while he drank and tried not to laugh at her enthusiastic if graceless movements. Tempting though it was to join her, he knew perfectly well that should he press his body close to hers he would feel compelled to drag her off to the bedroom for an hour. He thought it best to wait a while longer for that particular selfish delight.

Moments later, she kicked her shoes off with a shout of laughter and her movements became a little less robotic.

Shoes on or off, dance moves graceful or not, nothing could dim her beauty. Tonight she shone and, from the reactions that had followed her every move since the revellers had arrived, he was far from the only man to have noticed.

For only the second time since he'd met her, she'd abandoned her stock uniform of jeans and a shirt, in their place a beautiful white Bardot dress that exposed her slender shoulders and flared out at her waist to fall just above her knees. The beautiful chestnut hair had been set free from its usual ponytail to fall in tumbling waves over her shoulders and down her back. Subtle make-up and hooped silver earrings completed the feminine package. His heart throbbed every time he looked at her. Every part of him throbbed.

As if she could feel his gaze upon her, her eyes darted to meet his. There was a moment of stillness before the most beautiful smile lit her face. Spellbound, he continued to stare, the beats of his thumping heart the only sound he could hear, but then the spell was broken when Juan, his stable manager, swayed over to her, took hold of her hips and began to dance suggestively with her.

For the breath of a moment, the world seemed to go off-kilter. Thick heat filled his head while a nasty rancid taste filled his mouth.

Juan leaned forward to whisper in her ear. She smiled, shook her head and took a subtle step back, and Emiliano's world resettled... which was the moment when a pair of arms suddenly flew around his neck and a pair of pumped-up rouged lips parked an enormous kiss on his mouth.

'There you are,' Jacinda purred into his face. 'I've been looking everywhere for you.'

Concealing a groan, Emiliano disentangled her arms from his neck. Jacinda, a glamorously beautiful model, had married one of his team mates, Facundo, a year ago. At their wedding she'd trapped Emiliano in a corridor of the hotel the reception was being held in and come on to him like a rash. He'd firmly told her to sober up, to which she'd laughed and said she and Facundo had agreed to an open marriage. That hadn't particularly shocked him—he knew plenty of couples who enjoyed open marriages, but on her own wedding night? That just smacked of disrespect.

He'd done his best to give her a wide berth since then but she was like a fox hound, always sniffing him out, always trying to tempt him. Before, he'd always resisted out of loyalty to Facundo. Now, he found there was nothing to resist. Even if she hadn't been married to a man he considered a friend as well as an employee, he would have felt nothing apart from irritation that she was distracting him from watching Becky.

Fixing a smile to his face, he let her pull a stool against his and chatter away while trying to keep one eye on the dance floor. When she put her hand on his thigh he removed it without comment. When she did it a third time, his patience finally snapped.

'I think your husband's looking for you,' he said pointedly before getting off the stool and walking away.

He'd lost sight of Becky on the now crowded dance floor and had to crane his neck before he spotted a flash of chestnut hair.

To hell with it, he thought. There was no one else he wanted to spend time with. Why not dance with Becky? If they needed to slip off for a quick bout of lovemaking then so what? It was his party. They could do what they liked.

Before he could reach her, though, his polo team appeared with shot glasses. Together they drank to a successful season then drank again for luck to the new season, and then Nicky, his newest signing, waylaid him further by enthusiastically telling him about a young mare with exceptional potential he'd heard about that morning.

By the time Emiliano had extracted himself and reached the dance floor, Becky had gone.

Becky danced until her feet cried for mercy. And then she danced some more. She did not want to leave this dance floor. She didn't want to step outside and deal with the emotions she'd tried so hard to squash but were now threatening to erupt. This was a party. She needed to keep it together.

But it was getting harder to breathe. The air had become suffocating.

Not bothering to hunt for her shoes, last seen pilfered by a group of small children prancing around in them, she pushed her way through the heaving crowd and out onto the lawn.

She didn't know if she'd overheated from all the dancing but it felt even more stifling outside. She looked up and saw the thick clouds had finally reached them. The vast skies usually filled with twinkling stars had closed in on her too.

'Becky!'

Turning wildly, she found a handful of the grooms sitting on a wooden table drinking an enormous jug of cocktail through straws. She raised a hand in a wave then set off in the other direction, away from the crowds and noise. From the splashes and squeals echoing in the distance, a group of partygoers had decided now was the perfect time for a swim and, as she thought that, she remembered Emiliano saying he'd employed lifeguards for that very reason and increased her pace.

She didn't want to think of Emiliano. She didn't want to think of anything. All she wanted was a few minutes alone to breathe, pull herself together and then return to the party and carry on pretending that nothing was wrong.

She walked aimlessly, lost in thoughts she wished she could hide from until she found herself at the stables.

Usually a hub of activity by day, at night the stables were peaceful, allowing the horses to rest. She knew a couple of grooms had been unfortunate enough to draw the short straw to do the evening's night shift, just as she knew they would be given a substantial bonus by Emiliano for having to miss out on the fun.

She could scream. No matter where she went, there was always something that made her think of him.

Why hadn't she trusted her instincts and returned to England when she was supposed to? She could have spent the rest of her life in relatively happy denial.

Instead, she'd stayed and given her love for him air to breathe and now she was consigning herself to a life following in her mother's footsteps.

One day she was going to look at Emiliano and hate him, not as her mum had come to hate her dad for being the wrong husband but for breaking her heart. Because, marriage or not, Emiliano was going to break her heart.

And one day he would look at her and hate her too for forcing a promise of fidelity he would never have made if he hadn't wanted their child so badly.

A gentle neigh filled the air and Bertie poked his head out of the open part of his stable door. Walking to him, she stroked his kind head and was gratified when he nuzzled into her hand.

What wonderful creatures horses were. And how intuitive. But then she saw Bertie's stablemate, Don Giovanni, lying on the clean floor, barely bothering to conceal his disinterest at her presence, and stifled a laugh that could easily have turned into a wail if a large raindrop hadn't landed on her nose.

She looked up again at the dark, heavy clouds, and this time she did let out a wail.

More fat raindrops fell on her. Just as she was thinking she should take shelter in one of the empty stables, lights appeared in the distance. To her relief, they were headlights, and they were coming her way.

The pickup truck stopped feet away from her. She shielded her eyes from the glare of its lights and so couldn't see who was driving until it was too late and Emiliano jumped out.

'What the hell are you doing here?' he demanded as he strode towards her. 'I've been looking everywhere for you.'

She shrank away from the fury etched on his face and hugged herself.

'Everyone's looking for you!'

She wiped off another splatter of rain from her face. 'What for?'

Spitting out a curse, he pulled his phone out of his pocket, pressed the buttons quickly and put it to his ear. Eyes not leaving her face, he spoke rapidly into it.

'I've called the cavalry off,' he said tightly when he'd finished the call.

'I've only been gone twenty minutes,' she protested, bewildered at his anger.

'Lottie saw you walk off an hour ago!' he shouted.

An hour? How was that possible? But any

words she could have said in response would have been drowned by the heavens above them finally opening. In seconds she was soaked to the skin.

'Get in the truck,' he ordered.

But the emotions she'd fought so desperately hard to restrain suddenly erupted from her with the same force as the lashing rain. Heart pounding, emotions careering violently inside her, she took a step back and shook her head. 'Go back to the party. I'll join you when I'm ready.'

'Get in the damn truck or I will throw you in it.'

'Please,' she begged. 'Just leave me alone.'

Features as dark as the storm thrashing down on them, he took three quick strides to her, folded his arms across his chest and leaned down to snarl in her face, 'In the truck. *Now.*'

Anger suddenly punched through all the other emotions battering her and she snarled right back at him, *'Fine,'* before sidestepping around him and marching furiously to the truck. What other choice did she have? Either she got in willingly or he'd carry out his threat.

Emiliano's legs being so much longer than

hers, he reached the passenger door before she did and yanked it open for her. The moment her bottom touched the seat, he slammed the door shut then strode to the driver's side and climbed in beside her.

Without saying a word, he reached into the compartment behind the front seats and pulled out a towel, which he shoved onto her lap, then turned the vehicle's heating on.

An age passed where the only sound was the muffled deluge pelting the vehicle and their ragged, angry breaths.

Fury at being treated like a child overriding the despair that had brought her to the stables, Becky was loath to accept anything from him, but her wet skin was starting to feel chilled. Mutely, she rubbed the towel over her sopping hair then leaned forward to wrap it across her back and hold it tightly under her chin like a cloak.

'Ready to talk?' he asked roughly.

'I asked you to leave me alone,' she snapped. 'Why couldn't you respect that?'

'What, leave the mother of my child to catch pneumonia?'

And that was all he saw her as, she acknowl-

edged with angry pain even though it was confirmation of what she already knew.

He thumped the steering wheel in the silence,
making her jump. 'I want you to tell me why
you thought it was a good idea to abandon the
party to walk *barefoot* in the pitch-black in the
middle of a storm.'

She'd forgotten about her bare feet. Now he
mentioned them she could feel the sting, but
it was only a distant, dull ache.

'It wasn't raining when I left.'

'Anything could have happened to you!'

'On your private estate? Hardly.'

'Do you think scorpions care about boundar-
ies? Or snakes? Or spiders?' he snarled. 'This
isn't England. Our wildlife is dangerous. Damn
it, there was a report of a jaguar on land only
twenty miles from here recently.'

'I'm sorry if I caused anyone to worry,' she
said stiffly.

'Why did you go?' he demanded. 'I assume
it's to do with me from the way you just behaved. What made you do something so reck-
less and stupid?'

And, like a balloon deflating in one long
puff, her anger drained out of her. Emiliano

had every right to be angry. If he'd disappeared into the dead of night she would have been frantic.

'I really am sorry,' she said in a softer tone. 'I only meant to clear my head. I didn't realise I'd been gone for so long.'

Knowing he needed to get a handle on his temper, Emiliano pinched the bridge of his nose. He couldn't remember ever being so gripped by fear. He'd been worried when Becky had gone off for a ride on gentle Bertie but that had been nothing to the icy terror in discovering she'd disappeared into the black void.

'Just tell me why you left.'

'I saw you with that woman. At the bar.'

Gobsmacked, Emiliano stared at her, so many thoughts and emotions racing through him that it took a moment to separate them. 'You're talking about Jacinda?'

'I don't know her name. I'm talking about the woman who was all over you like a rash.'

'Then you are talking about Jacinda. She's married to Facundo.'

'She's married?' She covered her face. 'Does Facundo know his wife fancies you?'

'I have no idea.' But he had an idea of what Becky was implying. 'But let me assure you, when she couldn't keep her hands to herself I extracted myself from the situation.'

Just as he'd seen Becky neatly sidestep away from an amorous Juan on the dance floor. Had he assumed the worst? he thought angrily. No, he had not. Sure, there had been a tiny hint of something that could be construed as jealousy but at no point had that been directed at Becky herself.

He hadn't assumed the worst about Becky because he trusted her. It was a revelation that sucker-punched him.

'I know.' Her voice was devoid of emotion. 'I was watching.'

'If you know I gave her no encouragement, why run away?'

A fresh wave of pain-filled heat washed through her. The first time it had struck, Becky had been on the dance floor. She'd felt someone watching her and that someone had been Emiliano. The expression she'd seen on his face had cut through the noise of the music. There had been so much more than desire in that look. There had been tenderness too, enough to fill her heart with sudden hope. In that one tiny moment of time she'd thought she'd seen her own feelings mirrored back at her.

Which was why the pain of seeing her future had hit her so hard.

'Because I saw the day when you would *want* to give encouragement.' Jacinda had thrown herself at him and the smidgeon of foolish hope in Becky's heart had died.

'You think I would have an affair with a friend's wife?' he asked through tightly gritted teeth.

'No, I don't believe you'd do that but everywhere you go women throw themselves at you. Temptation travels with you.'

'Right, so you think I'm going to hook up with any woman who bats her lashes as me so long as she isn't a friend's wife? How many times have I told you? For as long as we're together, I will be faithful. Marry me and I will give you fidelity for life. What more do you want? For me to etch it in blood?'

'But that's just it.' She struggled to keep her tone even, every word feeling as if it was being dragged across a jagged blade. 'And that's why I can't marry you, even with that promise.'

His eyes snapped onto hers.

She tried to keep her words on an even keel but they fell from her lips like a runaway train. 'Sooner or later, all that's new and fresh and exciting between us will become stale and ordinary, but those women will still be new and exciting, and there are thousands of them scattered across the world, ready to bat their lashes and drop their knickers for you, and you will find yourself bound by a promise you never wanted to make. You said yourself you know it'll be a hard promise to keep! You'll want to act but your honour won't let you and then we'll be stuck in a marriage that's the worst of what our parents had—you'll be compelled to keep our deal just as your parents always stuck to theirs, but you'll come to resent me for tying you down and clipping your wings, just as my mother resented my father, and then that resentment will turn to hate and all that's good between us will be gone and our child will be the one to suffer for it.'

There was a long moment of stillness before he thumped the steering wheel again. '*Dios bendito*, you really do think the worst of me. You see a woman approach me and suddenly you're Nostradamus? You can predict my future thoughts and feelings?' His glare made her quail. 'You have a habit of doing that and it's never in my favour. Do you have any idea what that feels like? All my life, my father assumed the worst of me, my brother too, and now I learn that you...*you*, of all people...that your opinion *still* is no better than theirs. I have bent over backwards for you. I have treated you with respect and done my damnedest to compromise when others in my position would have used their wealth and power to ensure their child was in their care and under their protection, whatever the mother's opinion on it. I offer to marry you and when you run out of excuses you invent a future as an excuse.'

'I've agreed to move in with you when you return to England.' Her head was spinning again at the way the conversation had suddenly turned to be all about her. 'That hasn't changed.'

'Yes, it damn well has. You think I'm prepared to settle for crumbs? Live as a family for a few months each year but only when I'm in your country? Everything has to be on your terms. You'll have me begging like a dog to see my own child because your precious career comes before everything.'

'That's not fair!' she protested, her own fury regaining a foothold. 'I would never do that and how you can say that with a straight face when you refuse to consider retiring from a career where you've already achieved so much beggars belief. It's not as if you need to work any more—you have more money than a small country—but I've barely started and you want me to throw away all those years of work and dedication for someone who will never love or trust me because he's too stuck in the past to let it go.'

'You say *I'm* stuck in the past when you've just spouted all that prophecy rubbish?'

'None of which you denied! How can we have a real marriage without love? We *can't*, and without it we're doomed to repeat the mistakes our parents made. If you were ever capable of love and trust, Adriana stamped on it and the rest of your rotten family killed it. You're so damn cynical about *everything*. You don't want to marry me. You just want convenient access to our child.'

For the longest time they said nothing more,

the only sound in the truck's cabin their laboured breaths. The fury blazing from Emiliano's brown eyes would have scorched her if her own fury hadn't acted as a foil.

And then he whipped his gaze from her and, jaw clenched, turned the engine on. 'Put your seat belt on.'

CHAPTER FOURTEEN

REALISING EMILIANO WAS about to start driving, Becky hurried to obey. The moment her seat belt clicked into place, he did a sweeping reverse and set off, windscreen wipers on the fastest setting to fight against the deluge still pouring down.

In caustic silence, they returned to the ranch. He screeched the truck to a stop and got out, slamming his door behind him.

For the first time since she'd met him, he didn't do the chivalrous thing of opening her door.

Covering her head with the towel for protection from the rain, she hurried up the steps behind him. They both came to an abrupt halt at the noise that greeted them when he opened the door.

Much of the party had moved indoors, out of the rain. People were *everywhere*.

His eyes briefly found hers. He raised them, indicating they should go upstairs.

Ignoring the people trying to catch his attention, Emiliano climbed the stairs two at a time. Barney and Rufus spotted them and came bounding up to say hello before dashing back off to scavenge more dropped food.

Previous experience had taught him to lock his bedroom when he threw a party and it was something of a relief to get inside and close out the noise of revelry.

Becky hovered by the door, her beautiful green eyes wary. The soaking her dress had suffered had turned it transparent. Through it, her strapless white bra and matching knickers were visible. He wished he'd noticed before and warned her to wrap the towel around herself when they'd cut through the house. She'd be embarrassed if she knew.

Raising his gaze to the ceiling, he took a huge breath. 'Why don't you have a shower? You're soaked.'

She bit into her bottom lip before nodding and disappearing into the bathroom. He closed his eyes hearing the door lock behind her.

Alone, he stripped his own wet clothes off

and changed into a pair of jeans and a T-shirt. The adrenaline that had pumped so ferociously through his veins while he'd been searching for her, which had ratcheted up while they'd been shouting at each other in the truck, had gone. Feeling weary to his bones, he sank into the armchair and covered his face. His guts had tightened into a knot.

When she emerged from the bathroom with a towel wrapped around her, he averted his gaze while she slipped into the dressing room.

His heart squeezed when she joined him, dressed in her usual jeans and a check shirt but still as ravishing as when she'd been dressed so beautifully. She was limping.

'Are you hurt?' he asked.

She gave a rueful smile and perched on the sofa. 'My feet. Going for a walk in the dark barefoot was not my brightest idea. I've cleaned them and put antiseptic on the cuts.'

'Good.' He nodded his head and fought to keep all the thoughts that had raced through it while she'd showered in one place. 'I will arrange a flight back to England for you to-morrow.'

Her shocked gaze shot straight back to him. '*Tomorrow?*'

'It is for the best,' he said heavily.

'Why?'

'Because you're right. We'll end up hating each other.' He ruthlessly pushed aside the memory of the cold sweat he'd come out in, imagining Becky alone and injured on his estate. 'If we don't end it now, it won't take years. We'll hate each other before the baby's born.'

'But...'

'Don't say another word,' he warned, getting to his feet, averting his gaze so as not to see how quickly the colour had drained from her face. 'We've both made very clear what we think of each other. There is nothing left to say. We're going to be bound together for the rest of our lives. I would prefer to do that without thinking poison of my child's mother.'

He didn't want to hate her. That night he'd come damn close.

She'd accused him of being stuck in the past. Maybe he was. Maybe they both were. But he'd opened himself to her as he'd never opened himself to anyone and she still rejected him and assumed the worst of him. She'd seen all of him and she didn't want it. If he wasn't so determined not to hate her, he would hate her for staying these extra weeks when she must have known all along her mind was set.

It was time to let her go, and let go of the stupid dreams he'd had for them. A man had his pride. He wasn't going to beg. It wasn't as if he loved her and her return to England would break his heart.

That he'd realised he trusted her... That was a good thing, he told himself grimly. A man should be able to trust the mother of his child. Even if she lived on a different continent to him.

And that she sat there now, mute, not denying his own prophecy for them...

Fighting back the nausea bubbling like a cauldron in his stomach, he rammed his hands in his pockets. 'I'm going back to the party. I'll find somewhere else to get my head down tonight.'

'Okay.' Her voice sounded very faint and small to his ears.

'I'll be in touch soon.'

This time she didn't even open her mouth to acknowledge him, just gave a faint nod.

It wasn't until the bedroom door clicked shut that Becky gulped for air. She couldn't breathe. Oh, God, she couldn't breathe.

Stumbling to her feet, she staggered to the nearest window and fumbled with the latch to open it.

The rain had stopped. There was a fresh breeze. It kissed her face as she breathed it as hard as she could into her frozen lungs.

Emiliano didn't want her any more.

She'd pushed him away. She'd thought the worst of him one too many times and he'd turned from her as he'd turned from his father and brother for doing the exact same thing. He was already on the brink of hating her.

She didn't want him to hate her. Never that. Not the man who'd made love to her as if she were a precious gem to be cherished, the man who'd become more precious than any gem in her eyes. He'd become her friend as well as her lover. She'd shared things with him she'd never shared with anyone. And he'd done the same with her.

They'd shared something special and that was what she needed to cherish now. The memories. Because he was right, she knew it in her breaking heart. They'd reached the end of the road. Her love had no currency with a man who eschewed love. And her love wouldn't protect her when the inevitable happened and he grew bored of her.

But God, please help her—the *pain*.

Not bothering to strip off her clothes, she crawled into bed and tried not to think of the dreamy lovemaking they'd shared in it only hours ago.

'He still wants you,' she whispered to the tiny life inside her as she hugged her belly. 'Don't worry, your daddy will love you and protect you always.' Of that she had no doubt. He would support Becky too. If she needed help, he would give it.

The only thing he wouldn't give her was the one thing she so desperately wanted. His heart.

When the car pulled up outside the ranch the next day, Becky, who'd been hovering by the front door waiting, sank to her knees and cuddled the dogs goodbye. 'You two be good,' she said as she kissed their heads. 'I'll miss you.'

They nuzzled into her dolefully. If she was to anthropomorphise, she'd say they were sad about her leaving. In truth, they'd been up all night vacuuming any titbit of food they could get their greedy mouths on and having a marvellous time being petted by everyone. When she'd come down that morning, stepping over sleeping bodies strewn here, there and everywhere, she'd found the dogs curled together in the kitchen, too zonked out to do more than open an eye in greeting.

She kissed them again, then froze when a pair of huge feet in thick-soled tan boots appeared in front of her.

A wave of dizziness hit her and she sucked in a long breath before saying a prayer for strength and carefully straightening.

She hadn't seen him all day. While the great clean-up had been going on, the cleaning team sweeping and polishing around snoozing bodies, Emiliano had been nowhere to be found. But he'd arranged her flight home from wherever he'd holed himself up and asked Paula to pass on the details to her. The two women had already said their goodbyes.

She dragged in another breath to see his bloodshot eyes and stubbly face. He'd obviously slept in his clothes. Possibly in a bush.

His hair had foliage of a sort in it. He must have really enjoyed his return to the party.

They stared at each other for the longest time before he rammed his hands into his jeans' pockets. 'Have a safe journey,' he said hoarsely.

She nodded and tried to smile. It was as impossible as speech.

'Let me know when you get home?'

Still unable to speak, she nodded again and opened the door. The sun shone so brightly it blinded her...or was that the flickering of her eyes from a body so choked that every single part of her felt paralysed?

Somehow she managed to drag her feet to the car.

'Becky.'

She stopped in her tracks, heart suddenly leaping.

He paused a few feet from her, jaw rigid and throbbing at the sides, muscular arms folded across his chest.

She was going to be sick. She could feel it building inside her...

'I want you to listen to me,' he said quietly. 'You have to stop using your studies and your work as a shield to hide behind. Make new friends. Enjoy your life. Everything will change very soon, so enjoy your freedom while you have it. Okay?'

She sniffed back the tears, managed a jerky nod and then, concentrating harder than perhaps she'd ever done, managed to find a smile for him to remember her by.

The next time they met she would be noticeably pregnant, her features subtly altered. Let him remember her as she was now. '*Hasta luego*, Emiliano.'

And then she got into the car and drove out of his life.

On the flight back, Becky was inconsolable. The tears would not stop falling. She kept her privacy pod up the entire journey and sobbed until she wore herself out and slept, only to wake and sob herself to sleep all over again. Fourteen and a half hours later, voice hoarse and eyes sore from all the crying, tear ducts pleading for a rest, she landed in the UK.

Emiliano had arranged for a chauffeur to collect her from the airport so the hour-long journey to her new Oxford home went without any hassle.

Then she stepped inside and it hit her all over again.

The furniture he'd ordered for her on that shopping trip that now felt so long ago had been delivered. She'd known it was being delivered here—she'd given Emiliano the address and her landlord's details—but it hadn't occurred to her that it would all be unpacked and set out for her. Or that the flat would have been freshly decorated and have a new carpet.

Emiliano had arranged this. If she closed her eyes she could see him on the phone, barking out his orders in that way he had that was both no-nonsense but with a tone that made people *want* to go out of their way to please him.

She traced her fingers over the sofa she'd fallen in love with before she'd seen the price and baulked. In her bedroom, filling it so that she doubted she'd be able to open the wardrobe doors fully, was the sleigh bed she'd thought she'd cooed over without him noticing. She'd actually enthused about a different, much, much cheaper bed. But he'd noticed.

He'd noticed everything, she thought in wonder when she drifted into the small kitchen and found the slow cooker, and a food processor she'd run her fingers over before moving on to something else as she'd considered it an extravagance she didn't need.

But it was when she pulled the freshly laundered bedsheets back that her tear ducts were pulled back into service after their hard-earned break.

The pillow on the left-hand side of the bed, the side she'd slept when she'd slept with Emiliano, had a bespoke pillowcase on it. A picture of Emiliano's gorgeous face was imprinted into the silk.

Crying and laughing simultaneously, she cuddled his face to her belly.

She could picture him perfectly, his face alight with glee as he went to the trouble of ordering it and imagining her reaction when she discovered it.

When, much later, she was in that semi-conscious twilight state between sleep and wakefulness, her last coherent thought was that he must have forgotten about the pillow. Because it was the playful jest of a gift from a lover who expected or at least hoped for a future.

Not from someone who was preparing to let his lover go.

* * *

Emiliano stared at the screen before him. His finger hovered on the call icon in the laptop's corner.

This was something he would have preferred to do in the flesh but the person he needed to speak to was on a different continent to him. Europe. England, to be precise. Had flown there with no intention of returning to Argentina.

He clicked the icon before he could talk himself out of it again.

Moments later, his brother's face filled the screen. 'Emiliano! Great to see you!'

He had enough feeling left in him to acknowledge the small kindling of happiness that the man he'd tormented for most of his life should greet him with such enthusiasm and strove to inject the same enthusiasm into his own voice. 'Great to see you too. How's England? I bet it's raining.'

But his attempt at cheerfulness didn't fool Damián. His brows knotted. 'What's wrong?'

Before he could answer, Mia appeared in the background. She was the reason for Damián's uprooting of his life. The actress he'd paid to play the part of his lover…he'd fallen in love with her. And she'd fallen in love with him. This video call Emiliano had made had no doubt interrupted their wedding planning.

Mia waved at him with a beaming smile. He managed to raise his hand to wave back.

Damián turned from the camera to speak to her in a low voice. She looked briefly back at the screen before leaning down to kiss him, waved again at Emiliano and then walked out of the camera's range.

He heard a door close before Damián's face reappeared before him. 'What's wrong?' he asked again.

It took a few moments for Emiliano to gather his prepared thoughts back in order. Something about the way Damián and Mia interacted had knocked his thoughts off course, set off a tightening in his chest…

'Emiliano!'

With a snap back to attention he stared into his brother's concerned eyes and realised he was making this call for *her*. To swallow his pride and put the past behind him once and for all. Just as she'd told him to.

'There's something I need to tell you.'

'Oh?'

'About what happened during my time at the Delgado Group. With the money.' And then he took a deep breath and for only the second time revealed how he'd been played for a fool by a gold-digging con-artist.

Later that night, alone in his bed, Emiliano stared at the ceiling. The cliché of weights being lifted from shoulders was, he'd discovered, a cliché that was true.

He'd confessed everything. And then he'd apologised. For everything, including treating his younger brother like dirt for almost his entire life.

And Damián had apologised too for his own part in everything. They'd talked for hours. By the time they'd ended the video call, both of them had sunk half a dozen bottles of beer.

The weight of guilt he'd carried all these years had gone. The past was, finally, in the past and it would stay there.

So why did he still feel so heavy and lethargic?

CHAPTER FIFTEEN

AFTER THE NOISE and exuberance of Argentina, Becky had thought she would find it soothing to be back in such a quietly serious environment as a laboratory, a return to normality that she would easily settle into. And maybe she would have done if she didn't return home to her lonely flat every evening.

Last night, though, she'd gone for a meal with her new colleagues. She'd been touched that they were ready to include her in their social gatherings so soon and, remembering Emiliano's words about making new friends, had readily accepted. She'd enjoyed a good meal and even managed not to think about him for a few seconds.

And now here she was, alone in the huge bed he'd bought her with two whole days of nothing ahead and only the pillow with his image for company. The flat felt so small, not because it was tiny compared to the ranch but because

Emiliano magnified everything with his presence alone.

She'd been back in England for thirteen days. It felt like thirteen months.

She wondered if he was awake yet. The first polo competition of the Argentine season would be taking place later that day. She imagined him supervising the loading of his horses into the transporters that would drive them to the venue. She imagined the bustle and noise involved with transporting the minimum of ten horses he would personally ride that day, all the equipment needed, the grooms and other staff rushing around making sure they hadn't forgotten anything, and felt an enormous pang of regret that she wouldn't be there to share the day with them and that she wouldn't be there with the boys at her heels, cheering the Delgado team on until her voice grew hoarse.

The morning drifted away from her. Just as she was contemplating fixing herself something to eat, her doorbell rang.

How exciting. Her first visitor. Except she was expecting a book delivery, so the first person to arrive at her door would be the delivery driver.

But it wasn't a delivery driver standing on the doorstep.

It was her mother.

Emiliano watched the shadows on the bedroom walls. They'd been changing with the rising sun. Thinning.

He felt as if he was thinning too. Losing substance.

He'd thought putting the past to bed with his brother would snap him out of his bad mood but he only felt worse.

Becky had been gone for thirteen days.

His alarm went off. Rufus and Barney woke and jumped on the bed, slobbering over him.

They missed her.

He remembered Adriana, how frantic he'd been when she'd disappeared. He'd believed himself in love with her but he'd never felt that every breath taken was for her. Within days of her disappearance he'd shocked himself with how little he actually missed her. He'd thought about her constantly but only because of the question of where the hell she was.

He knew exactly where Becky was, but she was in his head every waking moment. She flooded his dreams—dreams that turned into living nightmares when he woke to find her side of the bed empty and he had to go through the grief process all over again, day after day.

To say he missed her would be like saying the sun was nothing but a yellow ball in the sky. There was a gaping hole in his chest filled with a pain so acute that it hurt to breathe and finally the truth penetrated his thick, stubborn head.

He loved her.

If he'd paid any attention to his feelings, he would have known the truth a long time ago. He'd fallen in love with Becky the moment he'd looked up from the trembling coward on the floor who'd dared kick his dog to see her holding Rufus so protectively in her arms. There had been no one for him since.

All these years spent actively avoiding commitment, going through women too quickly for them to feel the slightest hint of cosiness with him, cynically determined never to be fooled again by anyone, man or woman, driven by the sole ambition to prove that he was the best and that the whole world—his father and brother especially—should know about it, living his life with his own pleasures and needs at the centre of everything...

He was glad to now have his brother in his life *as* a brother, but nothing else mattered a damn.

He would give it all up for her. For Becky. The woman who'd stolen his heart, who made his world better with a simple smile. The woman with the tenderest heart. A woman he would trust with his life.

But a woman damaged. The years she should have spent drinking too much and having fun, having sex with her peers, had been lost as she'd wrestled with her parents' bitter divorce, which had culminated in her father's desertion and her mother's rejection, burying herself so deeply in her studies that she used it as a shield to protect herself from more hurt.

In his heart, he knew there would never be anyone else. If he couldn't have Becky then he would have no one.

He had to try. He knew that now. Maybe it was too late for them but he would try. He would get this competition done with and then he would fly to England, swallow his pride, get on his knees and beg for another chance.

Because he'd been the one to end things. She'd refused to marry him but at no point had she said she wanted to end their relationship.

Trust had to be earned. When had he ever given her the chance to trust his vow of fidelity? He'd been so damn intent on keeping control of himself and control of his feelings that he'd made it sound as if he was giving that promise as a sop to her, like some stupid benevolent gift, when the truth was he didn't want anyone else because there couldn't *be* anyone else. He was Becky's, heart, body and soul.

And if it was too late then at least he would always have a part of her. Their baby. He would stay in England and, living together or apart, they would raise him or her together and lavish them with so much love that they would thrive and grow up healthy and secure and with the ability to love and be loved.

He would have to be satisfied with that.

But he could do nothing about any of it right now.

With a kiss for his boys first, he climbed out of bed and dragged himself into the shower. He had to pull himself out of this funk. In an hour he'd be travelling with his horses and his team to the first cup competition of the season. He needed to be sharp. He needed his wits about him. Polo was too dangerous a sport not to be on form.

Five hours later and the doorbell rang for the second time. This time, it was a delivery of Chinese food for Becky and her mother to share.

The shock and disbelief she'd experienced when she'd first opened the door had slowly seeped away as the awkwardness dissolved and they began to talk.

Anthony, her sex pest stepfather, was history. Her mother had woken a few days ago after a dream about her unborn grandchild. It had been her epiphany. Her only child was pregnant and she didn't even know who the father was or when the baby was due. When she'd idly mentioned this to her new husband, along with her intention to arrange a meeting with her estranged daughter, his reaction had been so over the top and incredulous that suddenly the veil had slipped from her eyes.

It was as Emiliano had predicted. Having

taken his advice to keep the door to her mother open, Becky had messaged her new address the day she'd arrived back in England. Never had she believed her mother would turn up on her doorstep within two weeks of her sending it.

'Have you told your dad about the baby?' her mum asked after swallowing a huge forkful of *chow mein.*

Becky pulled a face. 'Not yet. He messaged last Wednesday. He was about to catch a flight to Chile to start his tour of South America. I'll tell him when we next speak.'

'Doesn't Chile border Argentina?'

She shrugged. She'd told her mum only that the baby's father was an Argentine polo player. It was too soon to start exchanging real confidences. Things couldn't return to how they'd been. Not yet.

'I bet your dad comes home for the birth,' she predicted.

Becky raised a brow in surprise at a comment about her father that was remarkably free of malice.

Her mum smiled ruefully and stabbed at a piece of sweet and sour chicken. 'I can't stand the man but he loves you. He was always a great father. He's dreamed of travelling the world since he was a kid. He put all his dreams on hold because he loves you and you needed him. He waited until you didn't need him any more.'

'I never knew that.'

'Well, now you do.'

'He never said goodbye when he left.'

'That's because he's selfish and immature.'

'I thought you just said he was a great father.'

'He was. And now he's a terrible one. Just as I've been a terrible mother in recent years.'

'I've hardly been the best daughter,' Becky admitted wretchedly. 'I'm a woman in my twenties expecting my parents to still put me first. If anyone's been selfish and immature, it's me.'

Emiliano had put her needs first, in all ways. Those weeks when they'd been lovers, he'd given her passion but also a security she'd never known.

'Becky?'

She blinked. 'Sorry, did you say something?'

'You looked lost in thought.'

The urge to spill all bloomed inside her. To

confide how desperately she'd fallen in love and how it had been her own distrust and lack of confidence in herself that had destroyed them.

All those things she wished she could have said to him. Things she *should* have said. Like how wonderful he was. How he made her laugh harder than anyone in the world. How he infuriated her more than anyone in the world. How he was also the best person she knew and how glad she was that he was the father of her child. Their child could have no better protector and guide.

'Becky!'

She jumped at the sharpness in her mother's tone.

Eyes that were a mirror of her own softened. 'Talk to me, honey. Please. I might be able to help.'

Tears filled her eyes. The urge to confide had grown big enough to choke her but, before she could open her mouth, her phone rang. She would have ignored it if the name of the caller hadn't flashed on the screen. Louise. Who should be busy tending the horses during the ongoing cup competition, not taking time out to make a call.

Fear immediately clutched her heart and it was with a hand that had turned to ice that she answered it.

'What's happened?' she whispered.

'Becks…' A large intake of breath. 'I'm really sorry to call like this but I thought you'd want to know. There's been an accident. It's Emiliano… He's had a bad fall on Don Giovanni. They crashed into…'

'How bad?' she interrupted.

'He's been rushed to hospital. He's not conscious. They think there's bleeding in his brain.' Her voice dropped. 'Becks…it's really bad.'

By the time Becky landed in Buenos Aires, thirty-six hours had passed since Louise's call. Her mum had already been on her feet, putting her handbag over her shoulder, when the call had finished.

'Where do you need to go?' she'd asked.

'Argentina.'

'Get your passport.'

Four minutes after the call to Louise ended,

her mum's car was screeching out of the parking space and pelting to the airport. Once there, she'd taken full charge. She'd bought Becky the first available ticket to Buenos Aires then, because the flight was twelve hours away, checked them into an airport hotel. For hours they'd lain on a lumpy bed watching rubbish on the television. In all that time Becky had hardly spoken. She was simply too numb to form a sentence, too numb to think coherently and too terrified to close her eyes to sleep. The hand not clutching her phone for news that didn't come had kept a tight grip on her mother's.

The long night had passed with agonising slowness. The wait to board the plane had been excruciatingly slow. The flight itself was purgatory. She couldn't even check her phone for news of his condition.

And then the plane landed and adrenaline kicked in. First to disembark, she was first at passport control too. With no luggage to collect, she ran straight to the exit, eyes glued to her phone as she waited for the messages she knew would have been sent from Louise and Paula during the long flight to ping through...

But disaster struck. Her phone died in her hand. She'd run out of battery and in the panic to get out of her flat and get to him she'd forgotten to bring a charger.

Stuffing her fist into her mouth, she screamed. She screamed for so long that when she finally pulled her hand out the sections of her fingers beneath the knuckles were bleeding from where her teeth had cut into them.

Not caring about the pain, she jumped into a cab and asked for the hospital. But she couldn't tell the driver which one. She didn't know! She knew the polo competition had been held in Buenos Aires itself so it had to be in the city. In desperation, she cried, 'Emiliano Delgado!'

To her horror, the driver immediately made the sign of the cross and put the car into gear.

Her brain turned to ice. Every part of her body began to shake.

She was still shaking when they arrived at the hospital, and when she saw the crowds of press outside her fear turned to terror.

Somehow she managed to fight her way through them but her battle was just beginning because no one—no one—would help her or tell her anything about his condition. They wouldn't even confirm if he was there!

But she knew he was. Why else would the press be camped outside? Emiliano had something akin to rock star status in Argentina.

Resolve filled her and she determined to find him herself. She didn't have to search long. At the far end of a long, wide corridor on the hospital's ground floor stood two security guards in front of a double door.

She ran to them. 'Emiliano Delgado?'

In unison, they folded their arms across their meaty chests and snapped at her in Spanish.

'English,' she beseeched, pointing at herself.

The taller one leaned down to speak in her face. 'Go 'way.'

'Please,' she cried. 'Just tell me if he's here and if he's alive. *Please.*'

'Go 'way.'

'No!' Too distraught to be intimidated, she shook her head vigorously. 'I no go.'

The smaller one scowled and spoke into a walkie-talkie. He'd hardly finished speaking when another security guard appeared and strode straight to her.

'You have to leave, miss.'

Turning her back to the door, she clasped her hands together and placed them to her chest. 'Just tell me how he is,' she begged.

Although he kept his tone pleasant, there was an edge of exasperation to it. 'I am not allowed to say. We have our orders.'

'*Please?*'

'You must leave or we will have to make you leave.'

Finally reaching the end of her tether, she clenched her hands into fists and shouted, 'I'm not going anywhere until someone tells me how he is!'

'Miss...'

'Just tell me if he's alive! You can do that! *Please!*'

'I cannot, just as I could not tell any of the others. Now...'

'Damn you, I'm not one of his *groupies*! I'm having his baby! Now, either you tell me if the man I love is alive or I'm going to...'

'Becky?'

Spinning round, she came to a stumbling stop. The double doors had opened and between them, sitting in a wheelchair in a pair of shorts and a T-shirt, was Emiliano.

CHAPTER SIXTEEN

EMILIANO BLINKED A number of times to make sure his concussion hadn't caused him to hallucinate.

But no. It really was Becky making all that racket outside his private hospital suite. It really was Becky who'd just shouted in the face of a man twice her size. It really was Becky who'd just screamed that she loved him...

Her eyes locked onto his and widened into orbs. Her trembling hands flew to her mouth and then reached out as she moved like a ghost towards him.

Silent tears streaming down her face, she tentatively placed her shaking fingers to his cheeks.

A burn stabbed the back of his eyes and he swallowed hard to ease his constricted throat.

While she explored his face with her shell-shocked eyes and gentle touch, Emiliano soaked her in too. His heart clenched and released over and over as he took in the exhaustion on her beautiful face, her crumpled clothing and hair that looked as if it had never seen a brush.

'*Is* it you?' He raised a hand to touch *her* face, still unsure whether she really was there or if he *was* hallucinating. Had he fallen back into one of the dreams that had plagued him in recent weeks, ready to turn into a nightmare any moment when he awoke?

Tremulous plump lips tugged at the sides as she gave a jerky nod but then her face crumpled beneath his touch and the tears turned into sobs that sounded as if they were wrenched from her very soul.

The emotion in his heart exploded. Hooking an arm around her waist, he pulled her onto his lap and held her tightly, burying his face in her hair and praying as hard as he'd ever prayed before that this was real.

Tears soaking his T-shirt, she curled up into him and held him as tightly as he held her.

'It's okay,' he whispered into her hair. 'It's okay, *bomboncita*. I'm here.'

Slowly she disentangled her arms and adjusted her weight so she could cup his face and stare deep into his eyes.

He smoothed a lock of her hair and stared back in wonder. 'I can't believe *you're* here. How did you know?'

'Louise called. I got here as fast as I could.' Her voice broke. 'I've been so scared. I thought...' Her breaths shortened, chest hitching under the weight.

'Thought what?' he asked gently.

'That you were...' Becky squeezed her eyes shut, afraid to even whisper what her deepest fear had been.

'That I was dead?'

Every cell in her body spasmed in agony to hear it vocalised.

'Becky, look at me,' he commanded quietly. His warm hands caressed her face in tender motions.

She gulped some air in and forced her eyes to open but before he could say what was on his mind, a doctor appeared. She stared at them with incredulity then spoke rapidly, clearly telling them off.

Suddenly, Becky realised she was curled up on Emiliano's lap. While she'd been overwhelmed with relief that he was alive and conscious, it had totally bypassed her that he must be seriously injured to be in a wheelchair. Horrified, she tried to stand but his hold around her tightened.

'You're not going anywhere,' he murmured into her ear before addressing the doctor in their native language.

The doctor's lips tightened but she nodded and indicated to one of the security guards who'd been watching the whole thing in stunned amazement. The guard pushed the wheelchair back through the doors and wheeled them to Emiliano's private bedroom.

Alone, they stared at each other again, faces so close the tips of their noses brushed.

'How badly hurt are you?' she whispered.

'Kiss me and I'll tell you.'

'Emiliano...'

'You cannot fly across the world to my deathbed without kissing me.'

She shuddered.

'I'm not dying. Not even close.' He gathered her hair together in a fist and tilted his head. 'Now kiss me.'

Heart hammering, she inched her face closer, closed her eyes and pressed her lips to his.

Neither of them moved. Lips joined, they breathed each other in. The scent of Emiliano's skin and feel of his firm, sensual mouth against hers gradually seeped into her senses, creeping through her veins and slowly filled her with such joy and such relief that she cracked, and suddenly they were kissing with the desperation of two drowning sailors who'd found a last pocket of air.

She knew the dazed look in Emiliano's eyes when they finally came up for air was mirrored in hers.

Hands sweeping through her hair, he smiled and pressed his lips to hers again. 'Help me onto the bed?'

Smiling back, she wriggled off his lap and held a hand out to him.

His movements were heavy and awkward as he heaved himself from the wheelchair and twisted to rest his bottom on the bed.

When he was finally sitting on it with his legs stretched out, he patted the space beside him. Already missing the feel of being pressed so tightly against him, she climbed up and cuddled into him.

'Why do you need the wheelchair?' she asked softly as their fingers laced together.

'Bruised spine.' He grunted a laugh. 'Bruised everything.'

'Louise said you had a bleed on your brain.'

'Suspected bleed,' he corrected. 'I was given full body scans. Nothing broken. Just a nasty concussion and bruising.'

'How's Don Giovanni? Was he hurt?' She knew he'd be more concerned about his horse than anything else.

'Not a scratch on him.'

'Good... What happened?'

'I don't remember. I was knocked unconscious. The first I knew I'd been in an accident was when I woke up in this bed.'

She shuddered again.

'But I know what caused it.'

She tilted her face to his. 'Oh?'

'And I know it will never happen again.'

'How?'

'I'm retiring. As of now. I'll find a player to replace me and I'll still finance the team but I won't play any more.'

'But *why*? You love playing.'

'Not as much as I love you and our baby. It's you I need to be with and that's what I'm going to do... If you'll have me and let me share your life.' His eyes shone with an emotion that burned. 'Since you've been gone my concentration has been shot. I've lost my focus and, as my accident proved, polo is too dangerous a game to play without one hundred per cent focus, not just for me but for the other players and my horses. If Don Giovanni had been hurt I would never have forgiven myself.'

She didn't hear anything after his first few words. Raising herself, she gazed down at his face, almost afraid to hope. 'You *love* me?'

He palmed her neck and expelled a deep breath. 'I've loved you since the day I met you, and if these last weeks have proven anything it's that I can't live without you. I can't. The morning of my accident I made a vow to myself that I would fly to you and beg for another chance. If not for the accident, I would have come to you. There has been no one else for me since the day I met you and there never will be. I need to be with you. Nothing else matters. Only you, and if I have to spend the rest of my life gaining your trust then I'll take that, so long as you love me…and you do love me…don't you?'

His sudden vulnerability made her heart full to bursting. 'More than anything. You're my whole world.'

'I know you don't want to marry me, but will you…'

'I *do* want to marry you,' she interrupted gently, placing a finger to his lips. 'I'm yours, body and soul.'

He closed his eyes and took a few deep breaths. When his eyes opened again, they were filled with such wonder it made the emotion in her bursting heart spill over.

'I cannot tell you how badly I have wished for this,' he said hoarsely. 'I swear I will never give you reason to doubt me. I will do everything in my power to be a good husband to you and a good father to our baby.'

'I know you will,' she said, replacing her finger with her lips. 'And Emiliano, I've never doubted you. It's myself I doubted. I didn't trust that your feelings for me could sustain a lifetime because I'm an insecure fool.'

'But I didn't help.' His eyes blazed with

self-recrimination. 'If I hadn't been burying my head in the sand and denying my feelings for you, I would have made the promise to be faithful without making it sound like I was doing you a favour. I buried my head in the sand rather than face the truth, and the truth is there has been no one else for me since the day I met you and there will be no one else but you for as long as I draw breath.'

'Even if you'd made the promise to be faithful without it sounding like a favour I wouldn't have believed it,' she said softly. 'I was too raw inside. I *did* shield myself in my studies and I didn't even realise, and I didn't realise I was running away from my hurt. You...' She sighed. 'Oh, you wonderful man, you've brought me to life and now my life is yours. I love you.'

And as she gazed into the clear brown eyes she loved so much she saw his love for her reflecting back at her and when their lips fused together she felt a rush of blood, knowing her heart would always beat for this man and that the blood in his veins would always flow for her.

* * *

Ten minutes later, the doctor opened the patient's door, having psyched herself to go in there and kick the visitor out. Really, this was not on. She didn't care how rich or powerful the patient was, he had a severe concussion and bruising and needed to rest, not be cavorting with women.

But then she saw the two fully dressed figures entwined on the bed and she stopped. The visitor's head rested against the patient's chest, the patient leaning into her, holding her protectively. Both were fast asleep.

There was something so symbiotic about the way they held each other that her breath caught and she sighed at the love she could feel enveloping them.

Hardly daring to breathe in case she woke them, she backed out of the room and softly closed the door.

EPILOGUE

'REPEAT AFTER ME. I, Emiliano Alejandro Delgado, take you, Rebecca Jane Aldridge, to be my lawful wedded wife.'

'I, Emiliano Alejandro Delgado, take you, Rebecca...' Emiliano suddenly paused and mouthed, *Rebecca?* to the woman he was in the process of marrying.

She nodded, her face turning bright red with suppressed laughter.

'Take you, Rebecca Jane Aldridge, to be my lawful wedded wife.'

'To have and to hold...'

Once they'd exchanged their vows and their rings—there had been one heart-stopping moment when Damián, his best man, had patted in the wrong pocket for them—and been pronounced husband and wife, they followed the priest with their two witnesses, Damián and *Rebecca*'s mother, to a private part of the church to sign the official document.

'Rebecca?' he whispered in her ear as he squeezed her bottom.

It was the only part of her he could currently squeeze as she was eight months pregnant. Their honeymoon would be spent on their English estate. Once they judged the baby to be old enough to travel, they would be moving back to Argentina, the place they both agreed felt more like home than anywhere else. Rebecca had a job lined up at an English-speaking research company close to the ranch, doing something similar to her current job with much reduced hours.

'You never did read my résumé, did you?' She sniggered.

And it was with the pair of them in fits of laughter that they signed the document that tied them together for the rest of their lives.

* * * * *

LET'S TALK

Romance

For exclusive extracts, competitions
and special offers, find us online:

f facebook.com/millsandboon

⊙ @millsandboonuk

🐦 @millsandboon

Or get in touch on 0844 844 1351*

For all the latest titles coming soon,
visit millsandboon.co.uk/nextmonth

Want even more
ROMANCE?

Join our bookclub today!

'Mills & Boon books, the perfect way to escape for an hour or so.'

Miss W. Dyer

'Excellent service, promptly delivered and very good subscription choices.'

Miss A. Pearson

'You get fantastic special offers and the chance to get books before they hit the shops'

Mrs V. Hall

Visit millsandbook.co.uk/Bookclub
and save on brand new books.

MILLS & BOON